SPECIAL MESSAGE TO READERS

THE ULVERSCROFT FOUNDATION
(registered UK charity)

Founded in 1972

research, diagnosis and treatment of eye diseases.
Examples of major projects funded by
the Ulverscroft Foundation are:-

- The Children's Eye Unit at Moorfields Eye Hospital, London
- The Ulverscroft Children's Eye Unit at Great Ormond Street Hospital for Sick Children
- Funding research into eye diseases and treatment at the Department of Ophthalmology, University of Leicester
- The Ulverscroft Vision Research Group, Institute of Child Health
- Twin operating theatres at the Western Ophthalmic Hospital, London
- The Chair of Ophthalmology at the Royal Australian College of Ophthalmologists

You can help further the work of the Foundation by making a donation or leaving a legacy.
Every contribution is gratefully received. If you would like to help support the Foundation or require further information, please contact:

THE ULVERSCROFT FOUNDATION
The Green, Bradgate Road,
Leicester LE7 7FU, England
Tel: (0116) 236 4325

website: www.foundation.ulverscroft.com

OUT OF THE NIGHT

One headless body, on the beach near
Frank Doy's home on the Cleveland coast,
was regrettable, two more were disturbing.
But when an uncommunicative woman
arrives at his house in the dead of night,
only to disappear again, Doy is involved in
something worrying. His search for her
uncovers a mysterious man with a private
art collection and some Russian émigrés.
Led deeper into the strange events
occurring in Port Holland and nearby
Meridion House, Frank tries to unearth
the secrets surrounding him and save the
life of his desperate female visitor . . .

Books by Dan Latus
Published by The House of Ulverscroft:

NEVER LOOK BACK
RISKY MISSION

DAN LATUS

OUT OF THE NIGHT

Complete and Unabridged

ULVERSCROFT
Leicester

First published in Great Britain in 2012 by
Robert Hale Limited
London

First Large Print Edition
published 2013
by arrangement with
Robert Hale Limited
London

A catalogue record for this book is available
from the British Library.

ISBN 978–1–4448–1606–8

Published by
F. A. Thorpe (Publishing)
Anstey, Leicestershire

Set by Words & Graphics Ltd.
Anstey, Leicestershire
Printed and bound in Great Britain by
T. J. International Ltd., Padstow, Cornwall

This book is printed on acid-free paper

For Sandra
who makes so much possible.

1

When they found the first body on the beach near Port Holland I didn't take much notice. I was busy at the time, tying up some work I'd been doing for a client who wanted to know why stuff kept disappearing from his hi-tech plant near Middlesbrough. It was obviously an inside job and I was on the brink of naming the supervisor with a nice little racket going.

Jimmy Mack said, 'It had its head cut off.'

I stared at him. 'What are you talking about?'

'That body they found.' He continued working away at a lobster pot he was mending. 'So they say, anyway.'

I shook my head. 'Ship's propeller, maybe?'

'Maybe.'

He didn't add anything, and I had plenty to do. So I left it there.

'I'll have to get back, Jimmy. I'm expecting a phone call. See you later.'

He nodded. 'There'll likely be more, you know.'

'More what?'

'Bodies.'

'Give over, you daft old bugger!'
I walked away in disgust.

* * *

The next morning I heard in the paper shop I visited that another body had been found on the beach at Port Holland. It seemed a curious coincidence, especially when the woman behind the counter shuddered and told the customer in front of me that the head was missing.

The third body was found not long after that. Headless again.

* * *

That was when Bill Peart came to see me. It was getting dark at the time. Mid-afternoon, and getting dark. That's what November days can be like at Risky Point, or anywhere else on the Cleveland coast. It's a different world compared to May time.

I saw the lights of his car as he picked his way cautiously up the long track that leads from the road to our cottages. Mine was the first one he came to. Fifty yards further on was Jimmy's.

That's all there is now at Risky Point. At one time it was a village, an ironstone miners' village, but there's not much left now. The relentless sea, and coastal erosion, has taken its toll. The only good thing is that at least the erosion has been gradual. Not like at Kettleness, a bit further south, where years ago the whole village slid into the sea in one go, and most of the population was saved only because there was an alum ship waiting offshore that managed to pick people up.

I knew it was Bill as soon as he opened the car door. I watched him get out, swing the door shut and then stand still for a moment. His weary, worn-out posture was what gave him away. Even in the gloom there was no mistaking those hunched shoulders, and I could already imagine that care-lined face. Nature and time had taken their toll on him, as they had on the coastal cliffs. I've never envied Bill his job, or his life. But he's a good man. Always was.

'You look like a man who needs a coffee,' I said, standing by the open front door.

'Better make it strong,' he said with an audible sigh as he came towards me.

He shook himself, as if dripping wet, and came inside. He really was wet, I realized then, although it wasn't raining.

'Take your coat off, Bill. Hang it up by the stove. What have you been up to?'

'Guess.'

3

'Headless bodies on the beach anything to do with it?'

He nodded and gave a weary sigh. 'As if I didn't have enough to do.'

I let him get settled while I made the coffee. It was a while since I'd last seen him, but we were old friends and sparring partners. From time to time he came over and we did a spot of fishing together. Or we just drank coffee and talked. As a serving cop, a detective inspector, he liked to keep an eye on what I was doing, and sometimes I got stuff from him. Sometimes we helped each other, usually unofficially.

'Bodies on the beach, eh?' I said, placing two mugs on the kitchen table and sitting down opposite him. 'Whoever would have thought it?'

He stared at me suspiciously. 'Is that you being funny?'

I smiled. 'Not really. What's going on?'

'No idea. It's not just heads that are missing either.'

'What else? Hands?'

He nodded.

That said something. Quite a lot, actually. It meant it hadn't been a ship's propeller. It was probably somebody who didn't want the bodies to be identified. Either that or it was an obscure message to others left alive.

With that grim reality hovering unspoken between us, we sat for a while, not talking much. It was warm in the kitchen, with the wood stove going full blast. I let Bill dry out and warm up a bit.

'Why is it your case, anyway?' I said eventually.

He looked at me.

'It's outside your patch, isn't it?'

Bill was with Cleveland Police. This was North Yorkshire. Just.

'How unlucky can one guy get?' he asked me. 'You're right, technically speaking, but . . . ' He shrugged. 'It's only just over the boundary, and the two chiefs did a deal for reasons best known to themselves.'

'So you're, like . . . seconded?'

'In a manner of speaking.'

'That really is bad luck,' I said with a grin.

He didn't respond. It was probably a sore point with him. Politics! I guessed he'd had the bad luck to be available.

'I've got something in the oven,' I said. 'Are you going to stay for supper?'

He looked up with interest. 'What have you got?'

'Lamb casserole. With rice, probably.'

He pursed his lips and nodded thought-fully. 'I could do, I suppose. I'll just get a bottle of wine out of the car.'

I smiled to myself while I waited for him to come back. The wine meant he'd planned this visit. Probably wanted to pick my brains. Well, good luck to him. He was welcome to anything he could find there. I knew nothing about headless, handless bodies on the Port Holland beach. Nothing to do with me.

That didn't mean I didn't want to know what Bill knew, of course.

2

I found out that Bill knew very little, seriously little.

'I haven't a clue,' he said when I asked him point-blank what it was all about. 'I got a call yesterday morning, and came straight down with a team. There wasn't anything at the scene for forensics and the tide was coming back in. So we did the necessary, recovered the body and then I packed everyone back off where they'd come from.

'Today I got another call. The same thing. Came back down. Recovered the body, and sent the team away. After that I hung around for a while, trying to get my head round what I'd seen.

'Then this afternoon it happened again. A dog walker — or his dog — found the third one. I was still in Port Holland. So I whistled my people back and they did the business.'

'Then you thought you'd come and see what your old mate Frank Doy has to say?'

'More or less. I was cold, wet, tired and hungry. Risky Point did seem like it might be a good place to come,' he admitted with a grin.

I thought about what he'd said. We were gently joshing each other but that was to keep things on an acceptable level. We had to be objective. Thinking too sympathetically about mutilated corpses could do your head in.

'Are there going to be any more?' I asked him.

'You tell me.' He shook his head impatiently. 'How the hell do I know?'

I felt like setting him on Jimmy Mack for an answer, but I didn't. Instead, I pulled the casserole dish out of the oven, checked the contents and began to set the table.

'Smells good,' Bill said, sniffing eagerly.

'You're only saying that because you've been on a wet beach in the cold all day. Wait till you taste it.'

He grinned and began to hunt for a corkscrew. 'Good stuff, this,' he said, holding up the bottle he'd brought. 'It's from the *Sunday Times* Wine Club.'

'The label should be worth reading, in that case. But what are the contents like?'

'Australian,' Bill said with a grin. 'Fifteen per cent.'

'Wow!'

'Exactly,' Bill said. 'Get through this, and we might come up with some fresh ideas.'

But we didn't. Not really. All we came up with was fantasy and speculation. Bill was disappointed, I think, that I had nothing to bring to the table but food.

'So you've heard nothing?'

I shook my head.

'No theories?'

'For God's sake, Bill! I've told you. I've heard nothing at all. I knew some bodies had been washed up, but that's all.'

'Washed up?' he said quickly. 'What makes you say that?'

I shrugged helplessly and sighed. 'They were on the beach. I just assumed . . . but I don't know. All right?'

Again, he was disappointed.

'Sounds like organized crime, though,' I said, trying hard to give him something useful to think about.

'Doesn't it?'

He yawned and stretched, and glanced at his watch.

'Do you want to stay tonight?'

He shook his head. 'Got to get back. But thanks for the meal.'

'Thanks for the booze. It's good stuff.'

'Isn't it? You finish it,' he added, draining the one glass he'd allowed himself. 'We'll do this again when I've got the case cracked.'

'In a couple of days' time, then?'

He just grinned.

* ★ ★

After Bill had gone I cleared up, checked my emails and texts, looked up the weather forecast, and went to bed. I was tired. It had been a busy day, and the end of an investigation that had been going on for a few weeks. I was glad to have finished it and placed the results in the hands of my client. It was up to him what he did with them. I was done.

The wind got up and I could hear the sea crashing against the base of the cliffs, and draining back through the boulders and shingle; the rumbling, hissing, seething sound you get with a high tide. I liked listening to it. I was used to it, and accepted it as part of where I lived, but it was still pretty awesome.

I was asleep a couple of hours, I subsequently worked out. Then I woke up. It was still dark and I was puzzled. Something had woken me but I didn't know what. I lay still, listening, feeling, waiting. Now I was awake I was on edge. Old habits. Conditioning. Something had woken me. I needed to know what it was before I moved.

Three or four minutes passed. Then I heard a sound that didn't belong. Even through the noise made by the wind and the sea I heard several dull thuds from somewhere downstairs, perhaps from outside. Not loud noises, but something different. I got up to investigate.

It was black outside when I looked through the window. I could see nothing. I put a light on and made my way downstairs, wondering if something had come loose in the wind. Downstairs seemed normal. Nothing there. I stood, listening. Then I heard it again. One thud this time, against the front door.

I put more lights on, unlocked the door and started to open it. Immediately, the door slammed heavily against me, forcing me back off-balance. I held on. The door kept on coming, and with it came a shower of icy rain — and a wet, naked body that hit me hard and sent me staggering backwards.

Automatically, I dropped into a crouch, prepared to fight, but the body was an inactive dead weight. So my fists relaxed and I reached out to grab and hold. Then I probably gasped with shock as I realized what I was holding on to: a naked woman who was extremely wet and cold.

'Help me!' she whispered. 'Please help me.'

3

She couldn't stand unaided. She was hanging on to me desperately to stop herself falling. I struggled to hold her upright. Somehow I managed to manoeuvre her far enough inside that I could slam the door shut with my foot. Got the wind and the rain out of my face.

'Please!' she stammered again, teeth chattering wildly, and her whole body shaking.

I lifted her off her feet and took her through to the living room. As gently as I could, I laid her on the sofa. It wasn't easy, and I was glad to be rid of her weight.

It was only when I straightened up that I could see her properly. She was young. Probably in her twenties. And she was completely naked and blue with cold. She pulled her arms across her breasts and held on, shivering uncontrollably, her legs jumping, her eyes shut tight.

'Stay there,' I said, virtually on autopilot. 'I'm just going to get some towels and a blanket.'

She didn't reply. She just lay there and shook hard enough to make the sofa rock.

I brought a big bath towel and covered her with it. She made no move to dry herself. She was too weak. So I did the best I could, as quickly as I could. Then I covered her with a quilt and turned my attention to the stove.

It was still quite hot. Briskly, I stirred the embers and placed some kindling on top of them. When they got going, I started piling in some bigger lumps of wood, all of it driftwood collected from the beach, none of it a sensible shape or length. But it took hold and began to crackle. I shut the door.

All the time I was processing what I knew of my visitor. It didn't take long. She was young, painfully thin and desperate, incredibly desperate. Inevitably, my thoughts jumped to the bodies that had been found on the beach. Should this have been another one? Had she somehow averted what had happened to the others? It seemed a strong possibility. Someone must have been after her. She hadn't got into this state all by herself.

Before I did anything else, I went to the cupboard under the stairs and took my shotgun out of its locked case. I placed it where I could easily reach it.

That done, I returned to the sofa. She stared up at me, still shaking but eyes wide open now.

'What happened?' I asked gently. 'Where have you come from?'

She said nothing. Just stared. In shock, probably. Either that or too cold for her brain or tongue to function.

'Can you tell me anything?'

'Thank you,' she said.

That seemed to be it. I decided not to press her for the moment. I was worried about her condition, as well as curious about how she had ended up here. She was probably suffering from hypothermia.

'I'll make you a hot drink,' I said, turning away. 'That'll help.'

'Thank you,' she said again, wheezing this time.

'Then I'll call an ambulance,' I added over my shoulder. 'Get some paramedics here to take you to hospital.'

'No!'

The cry startled me. I spun round and stared at her. She stared back, wide-eyed.

'We need help,' I said gently.

'No,' she said again. 'Please! They will kill us.'

'Who will?'

She just shook her head.

I considered for a moment. Then I said OK and went to make some coffee.

While the water was heating, I took a quick

look outside. Nothing. Nobody. Not in the immediate vicinity, at least.

She sat up to take the coffee mug from me. I was surprised by her powers of recovery. Minutes ago she hadn't been capable of that. She was still shivering, though. And still terribly cold.

'So what happened?' I asked her again.

She sipped her coffee and then put the mug down on the small table I had placed within her reach.

'I am sorry,' she said. 'I can tell you nothing.'

I nodded. 'OK.'

Foreign, I had decided by then. From her accent, European — probably.

'Lucky I heard you,' I said with a smile. 'Lucky I'm a light sleeper.'

She nodded. 'Thank you,' she said again. 'I thank you.'

'Where are your clothes?' I asked. 'Who was chasing you?'

She put down the coffee mug and her expression became blank. I was getting nowhere.

'All right, all right!' I raised my hands, palms out, to placate her. 'How do you feel? Can I ask you that?'

'Better, thank you.'

I was getting tired of her words of

gratitude. I wanted more from her. But I knew I wasn't going to get it yet.

'I'll find you some clothes,' I told her. 'You stay there and finish your coffee. And don't,' I warned, 'say 'thank you' again!'

An expression of alarm flashed across her face. She gazed at me warily. I smiled. She relaxed. 'You make joke,' she said.

'Small one,' I agreed.

★ ★ ★

I went upstairs and dug out a pair of jogging pants, a thick flannel shirt and a heavy-duty sweater. She was going to have to make do without underwear. Mine wouldn't fit and none of my visitors had left any behind.

I switched off the bedroom light and moved the curtain aside. Still a black, stormy night. I could see nothing. Here at Risky Point we have no light pollution whatsoever. An astronomer's paradise, apart from the rain, fog and cloud.

For a moment I stayed where I was. Who on earth was she? And what the hell was I going to do with her? One thing I knew: I looked forward to meeting whoever had got her into this state.

Then I smiled ruefully as one of Jimmy Mack's many criticisms of me came to mind.

16

I didn't need to go looking for trouble, he had once said. All I had to do was stay where I was, and it came to my door. This looked like more of the same.

She was lying down again when I went back downstairs, her coffee mug empty.

'Feel any better?'

She nodded, and managed to avoid using her stock phrase again.

'I've found you some clothes of mine. They won't fit but at least they'll keep you warm.'

'Thank you.'

'Would you like a hot bath first? That would help.'

She hesitated and then said she would. I helped her up and steered her to the stairs, still wrapped in the quilt. Somehow we got up them. Then I ran the bath while she watched.

'Can you manage now?'

She nodded. I hesitated a moment but decided she probably could. 'I'll bring those clothes up for you,' I said. 'You carry on. If anything is too difficult, give me a shout. My name is Frank, by the way.'

She nodded and actually smiled. Things were looking up.

After that I checked the bed in the spare room and threw an extra quilt on top. Then I returned downstairs and waited. A long soak would do her good.

A loud thump on the ceiling twenty minutes later suggested things were not going so well upstairs. I raced back up and found she had extricated herself from the bath but was now sitting in a heap on the floor, the towel wrapped around her.

At least the shivering had stopped. I picked her up with difficulty and carried her to the spare room, where I laid her down and covered her with the quilt again. I could see plenty of nasty scrapes and bruises on her legs, and her feet were a mess, but any serious bleeding had stopped.

She was almost asleep now. So I decided any further attention, let alone questions, could wait till morning. At least she was a bit better now, if battered and exhausted. She was out of danger. The resilience of youth.

But I wasn't sure I was OK. In manoeuvring my visitor around, something had gone pop in my back. So the best place for me, too, was bed.

Downstairs, I checked the locks, collected the shotgun and switched off the lights. Then I, too, sought refuge in sleep. I was tired and sleep didn't take long in coming.

I woke up about 7.30 a.m., my usual time in the winter months. It was just starting to get light by then. I lay still for a minute or two, recalling the events of the night, sorting my head out. Then I got up, pulled on a few clothes and went to check on my visitor.

She was gone. The bed was empty and cold.

4

I was shocked. Pulse racing, I started checking. The bathroom — empty. There was nowhere else upstairs. I ran downstairs. No sign of her. By then I was really worried.

I went through the cottage again, more carefully this time. There were no signs of a struggle, no signs of an abduction. I knew there couldn't have been anyway — I would have heard it. The bedroom, and the rest of the house, were simply empty.

All the windows were intact, closed and locked still. Both external doors were shut, undamaged and locked with the Yale locks. The back door was also fastened with a double cylinder, deadbolt lock. The serious lock on the front door was open. It had been opened with the key, which was still in place.

That was it. My inescapable conclusion was that she had let herself out and departed voluntarily. There was no other explanation. I opened the front door and took a quick look outside. No one there, and nothing unusual in sight.

Back indoors, I checked through the house once more and discovered that she had taken a few things with her. Not much, though. Just enough. Understandably, she had kept the clothes I had given her. She had also taken an old jacket that I kept hanging behind the front door and a pair of light-weight walking boots. The boots would be too big for her, like everything else, but she had to have something on her feet in this weather.

What the hell was going on? I swore savagely and slammed a door or two. It wasn't because of the stuff she had taken. That didn't matter. It was partly because this mystery that I didn't need had been dumped on me. It was even more because I feared for her. It's not often a girl has arrived on my doorstep in the middle of the night. Not uninvited anyway. And never in such condition.

Whoever she was, she was obviously in serious trouble of some sort. And now I was involved. I had seen her naked, touched her, carried her, helped her — and done my best for her. I was involved. I didn't want her to end up as another headless, handless body on the beach. There might not have been any connection at all between my visitor and what had happened at Port Holland, but I didn't believe that for a moment. She was in trouble.

I made some scrambled eggs and coffee for breakfast, and took my time over it. There was no hurry, and I needed to work out what I was going to do next.

Briefly, I thought about Bill Peart. Briefly. Bill was officialdom, and one thing the girl had impressed on me was that she didn't want the official world alerted. Given that she had sounded foreign, I suspected that was because she was here unofficially. Perhaps illegally.

So no Bill Peart.

I decided to look for her myself. It was possible that she had left Risky Point far behind, perhaps by hitching a lift, but it was also possible that she had not gone very far at all. I tried not to consider the possibility that I might find her at the foot of the cliffs, without her head, but I couldn't rule it out.

★ ★ ★

Risky Point is a strange, abandoned place, a ruined village on top of high cliffs that are constantly retreating. To the north is Boulby, with higher cliffs than anywhere else in England. To the south, more cliffs — all the way down to Whitby and beyond. Once a railway ran along the top of these cliffs. And at the base of them are countless industrial sites and relics, places where men have for centuries quarried and dug out a living from ironstone, alum shale and jet, as well as from fishing.

On top, too, there have been plenty of shafts and quarries dug by men mining the seams of iron ore that run through Cleveland. Often in these places, as at Risky Point, villages were built for the men who worked there and their families. Many survive still, communities where people now commute or eke out a living in ways that once would have been unimaginable. It's a strange, hard and yet still attractive landscape that is as impressive as any I know. It's also one with great opportunities for concealment, if you want to hide and stay hidden.

I started my search outside my own front door. To my relief, I didn't find a body in the first hundred yards. That strengthened my optimism. I pressed on.

It was a raw morning. The cloud was low and dark, and there was a biting wind coming off the sea, bringing with it flurries of needle-tipped sleet. I walked northwards first. I wasn't looking for anything in particular. I was looking for things out of the ordinary.

Most of all, I was hoping I wouldn't find a woman's body.

I walked north for a couple of miles and then turned round to come back and let the wind freeze the other side of my face. I kept on going until I reached our cottages, still with the same vague objective in mind. But I had seen nothing. In a way, I was reassured. Unless she had fallen over the cliff edge, which I was inclined to rule out, I was starting to believe she had managed to get well away. Somehow she had. Good luck to her. My mind was slightly easier, despite the enduring mystery. I hoped she had a good life, and a long one, ahead of her.

*　*　*

I called in on Jimmy Mack, just to say good morning. He was in a funny mood. Grumpy and bad-tempered. He didn't say much. He was in his shed, re-arranging his tools and generally being uncommunicative.

'You didn't see or hear anything last night, did you?' I asked him.

'Just the usual.' He turned to look at me. 'Why?'

I shrugged.

'Any more bodies yet?'

'I hope not. Bill Peart came over yesterday

afternoon. I think it's wearing him out already.'

'That's easy done, when you start finding folk without their heads.'

He shook his own head, as if he didn't know what the world was coming to.

'What do you think, Jimmy?'

'Me? I haven't made my mind up yet. But there's plenty going on around here. I can tell you that. We haven't heard the last of it, not by a long chalk.'

He wasn't feeling sociable and he didn't offer me coffee. He seemed determined to be enigmatic. So I moved on and walked a mile or two to the south. Still nothing. By then, I was pretty relaxed about the whole thing. I suspected it might be a long time, if ever, before the night's events were explained. I could live with that.

As I trudged northwards again the cottages came into view, about half a mile ahead. I saw a car travelling along the access track towards them. It stopped outside my place. Two men got out. One of them knocked on the front door while the other went round the back.

I broke into a run. By the time I reached my gate, one of them was inside my shed and the other was working on the lock on the front door. I yelled at the one on my front doorstep. He looked over his shoulder at me and then carried right on.

5

I yelled again at him, telling him to get away
from the door. He ignored me and carried
on.

I launched myself at him, grabbing him by
the shoulder and spinning him round. He
dropped into a fighting crouch and stabbed
the tool he was using at my face. I dodged
and stepped back off the step. He kept on
coming, his face a vicious snarl.

He was higher than me now. I stooped,
grabbed his lead leg and heaved it up. He
toppled backwards. I stepped in and
stamped hard with my heel on the hand
holding the tool. He grabbed my leg with
his other hand. I pulled back and kicked
out.

Then I was hit by a hurricane from behind.
The guy's mate had arrived. I slammed into
the wall with my face. Somehow I rolled
sideways and turned to meet him. He stepped
back and pointed a knife at me.

'Come on, then!' I snarled, enraged. I
brushed my face quickly with the back of my
hand, getting blood and grit out of my eyes.

He stepped back another pace but he

wasn't really backing off. He was giving himself space.

'You don't want trouble with us,' he sneered.

No more chat. I went for him, ducking and throwing a punch that fell short, moving from side to side. I wanted to get it over with before the other one was back on his feet.

But he kept moving away, holding the knife low in front of him, warding me off. I ducked and weaved, and kept going, crowding him, working to back him up against the stone wall.

Suddenly I had him. He was all backed up, nowhere to go. But it was too late. Out of the corner of my eye I had seen the first guy getting to his feet, and he was behind me. Well, the one with the knife was going down, whatever else happened. The fighting madness was in me now. I coiled, ready to spring.

An explosion tore through the air. I paused, shocked. But only for a moment. The guy with the knife turned sideways to look. I hit him hard, slamming his head against the wall. I grabbed his knife hand and banged his face into the wall again, hard. He dropped. But I kicked him anyway.

'That'll do!' I heard Jimmy Mack boom in his gravelly voice.

I pulled the knife free and spun round.

Jimmy had his shotgun at the ready, pointing at the first guy. The man had stopped moving and was weighing up his options, fists dangling by his sides.

I stepped away, doubled up for a moment to catch my breath and then straightened up again. I nodded at Jimmy. He had his elbows on the top of the wall, holding the shotgun rock-steady.

I kicked the one on the ground hard again, making sure he was out. Then I reached down to go through his pockets. Apart from the knife, which was a serious-looking, commando-style weapon, he carried only car keys and a thin wallet. The wallet contained fifty quid and a couple of bank cards. I kept it and threw the car keys at the other guy. They hit him in the face and fell to the ground.

'What were you after?' I demanded.

He stared at me with fierce hatred. 'You'll regret this,' he said. 'You'll live to regret the day you were born!'

American accent, I noted.

'I don't think so,' I told him. 'I really don't think so. What were you looking for?'

He glared at me with ferocity. I smiled back and considered what to do next. I could call the police, but how long would they take to get here?

And now the other guy was sitting up and

preparing to stand. Could we hold them long enough, without shooting at least one of them? And, if that, how long would police inquiries and the inevitable court case take? I could see the headlines now: 'Householder arrested and charged with grievous bodily harm, and attempted murder'. Would we live long enough to see it through?

Anyway, I knew pretty well what they were looking for. I didn't need them to tell me.

And they had been thwarted. If Jimmy hadn't been there I might have taken the chance to work on them and find out for sure. On the other hand, of course, if Jimmy hadn't appeared I wouldn't have had the chance.

'Get him in the car,' I said to the one still on his feet, 'and get the hell out of here.'

He glared at me.

'You don't frighten me,' I told him. 'You may not know who I am, but I can tell you now you've picked on the wrong man. I've come across a lot uglier pieces of shit than you. Now get moving before I change my mind!'

A last lingering look of pure hatred. Then he moved. He got his mate on his feet, and them both into the car. Then they took off.

We watched them disappear down the track. As their car turned onto the road,

Jimmy turned to me and said, 'What was all that about?'

I shook my head. 'It beats me.'

Then I relented. 'You came at just the right time, Jimmy. Thanks. Fancy a cup of coffee, or a thimble of something else?'

'It's a bit early for me,' he said slowly. 'For the coffee, I mean.'

I grinned and turned to open the door with a key, the way it should be done.

6

'You'll not know them fellows, I take it?'
Jimmy said, as he sat nursing his whisky at
my kitchen table.

'Never seen them before in my life.'

'Thought as much,' he said dryly. 'What
were they after?'

'Beats me.' I shook my head. 'Burglary?'

'They didn't run,' Jimmy pointed out.
'Pretty tough burglars.'

'Yeah.'

I wondered whether to tell him about my
midnight visitor. Instead I made coffee for us
both. He would drink it, whatever he'd said
about it being too early, and I needed it.

'I don't think they were from round here,
Jimmy.'

He kept whatever thoughts he had on that
subject to himself. He just nodded and
looked around with a fresh eye. 'I should fix
my place up like this,' he said. 'Nice curtains,
new furniture, and everything. And china,' he
added, turning his coffee mug round so he
could study the pattern on the side.

Made there, as well, I thought but didn't
say. I didn't want him turning the mug upside

down to have a look.

'It's all right, your place. What's wrong with it?'

He grinned. 'All right for me, you mean?'

'That's what counts, isn't it?'

I don't suppose Jimmy's cottage has been changed much since his parents passed away. It's still a fisherman's cottage, a time capsule. One of these days it will be discovered by a television company and hailed as a cultural relic of outstanding national significance. Not outstanding natural beauty, though.

'Don't forget, Jimmy. When you want to tackle that hole in the kitchen roof, let me know. I'll give you a hand. That polythene sheet won't last through another winter.'

He nodded. 'I'll let you know.'

'I could even do it for you, if you don't feel up to it. That's the least I could do for the man who's just saved my life.'

'Would it be done right, though?' he asked mildly, unimpressed by the flattery.

'Well . . . I replaced the whole roof on this cottage. It seems all right, doesn't it? Keeps the weather out.'

'We'll see. There's some funny things going on these days,' he added.

I looked at him, wondering where we were now.

'Bodies on the beach,' he said. 'Strange folk

around. Now this — gangsters.'

I digested that for a moment. 'You've seen other . . . people?'

'A few. I don't know where they're coming from, mind. But there's something going on.'

Something going on? Well, yes. Quite a lot, actually. He was right there. And I suspected he knew more than he was saying.

'You said yesterday there would be other bodies found — more than the three?'

He nodded and drained his glass. 'The beaches along this coast are funny places. Lots of nooks and crannies. Fisher folk have always known that. Why would three be all there is?'

Why, indeed. Why stop there?

But I wondered if he was just talking riddles now, and didn't know anything more.

'That's a big fancy boat, as well,' he added.

I looked at him.

'At Port Holland. Supposed to be a yacht, but it's not what I would call a yacht. More a rich man's toy. To me, a yacht has a sail, and goes with the wind.'

'To me, too,' I said gravely. 'Who does this boat belong to?'

'Some artist fellow. Foreign, I think. Plenty of money, anyway. Like that other one — Picasso, is it?'

'He's dead, Jimmy.'

'Is he now?' He looked surprised. Then he gave me a grin that suggested he was having me on. 'Well, you can't take it with you, can you?'

I was becoming impatient with the conversation. It was always the same with Jimmy. Instead of just telling you things straight off, he always had to wrap it up in mysteries and riddles. I could never decide whether he couldn't help himself or if it was for his own entertainment.

Still, it was an interesting bit of information he'd just given me.

'How's he got a big, posh boat in there? The old harbour's nothing but a demolition site.'

'He's fixed it up.'

'Oh?'

Port Holland had been built in the nineteenth century for ships to load iron ore from a local mine and take it to an ironworks and shipyard on the Tyne. The more modern story was that army engineers had blown the harbour up early in the Second World War to prevent the Germans using it as an invasion platform. It had remained a heap of rubble ever since, to my knowledge. But it was a while since I'd last been to have a look.

Jimmy shook his head and chuckled. 'He's spent some money on it! He certainly has.

You know what they're like, these fellows. Some of them buy a football club. This one's different. He likes the sea.'

I was wondering who he meant by 'these fellows', but not enough to be able to ward off fatigue indefinitely. I yawned. The events of the past day and night were catching up on me.

Jimmy looked round as a sudden squall rattled the windows. 'More sleet. It's going to be a hard winter, starting as early as this.'

'Probably.'

'Them two,' he added with a sly grin, 'the burglars? They were looking for something, I reckon, something they wanted badly. Before they came over here they went through my shed. They spoke to me, as well.'

I was astonished. 'They spoke to you?'

He nodded. 'They wanted to know if I'd seen a girl, a young woman.'

So I'd been right about what they were looking for. It was the girl they wanted. What the hell was it about?

'What did you tell them, Jimmy?'

'I told them no, I hadn't seen one. I hadn't been so lucky in a long while. In fact, I told them, it had been so long that I didn't really want to see one at all now. It's too late. It would be like winning the football pools after filling them in all your life without success.

What good would millions of pounds do me now?'

'What did they say to that?'

'Nothing. They just muttered amongst themselves.'

I grinned and looked in the coffee pot. Plenty left. I poured us both some more. It was time I told him something.

'Jimmy, I have a confession to make.'

He didn't seem surprised. 'I wondered about that,' was all he said.

So I told him about the girl. It wasn't fair not to, given how he had helped me — and how he might have put himself in jeopardy by doing so. He had a right to know what was going on. As much as I knew, anyway.

He didn't laugh or make any of the jokes I might reasonably have expected about a naked girl arriving on my doorstep in the middle of the night.

'So you went out looking for her this morning?' he said, having heard me out.

'I did. I didn't find her, though. To be honest, I was pleased.' I shrugged and added, 'It means she's probably still alive — especially if those two are still looking for her.'

Jimmy was quiet for a while. Then he said, 'What about the beach? Did you look down there?'

I grimaced and shook my head. 'I'm going

to have to, though, aren't I?'

'Aye. I think you'd better.'

We didn't say much more. Probably neither of us knew much more worth saying. Shortly afterwards, Jimmy went back to his own place. He was a loner. He couldn't take much company in one go, or any at all for more than a short time. I didn't mind his going. I needed to do some thinking, and to make some preparations. What I had in mind wasn't going to be easy, and I wasn't looking forward to it.

7

It was possible to get down from our place to the little beach at the foot of the cliffs, but it wasn't easy. The path was very rough and steep — part of what was left of a 'sailors' trod'. It started just past Jimmy's cottage and wound its way down to the small bay from which Jimmy and his forebears had always launched their fishing boats. In good, dry weather it wasn't too bad. In fierce wind and driving sleet, with the rock wet and slimy, it wasn't something I would normally do voluntarily. But circumstances were far from normal.

Before I departed I checked round the house again, part of me perhaps subconsciously wondering if the girl might still be here, tucked away in a cupboard somewhere. There was nothing to find. So I prepared to leave. Despite the weather, I made a point of opening a small kitchen window slightly on the leeward side of the house. It was still icy cold outside but a bit of necessary ventilation wouldn't lower the house temperature much. The stove would stay hot for a few hours now I'd closed it down to slumber mode.

I took with me a backpack containing a few sensible things: first-aid kit, survival blanket, a bottle of water and a flask of coffee, some high-energy food bars and a climbing rope plus a couple of karabiners. I hoped I wouldn't need any of them, especially the climbing gear. I also had a good torch, a whistle and a mobile phone that I knew worked sometimes down there. A dead body was one thing, but another possibility was that I would find a badly injured young woman.

The wind spotted me straight away and screamed in fury, trying to dislodge me from the track. I ducked my head and kept going, trying not to think of much beyond the next few steps. The outcrops of wet sandstone weren't too bad to negotiate, but in places there was nothing for it but to let go and slide down expanses of the slippery shale that constituted much of the cliff. Jimmy's ancestors had carved footholds here and there in times past but they weren't much use when they were covered in sleet and running water. Best — quickest at least — just to slide down the rock, and hope coming back up wouldn't be a problem.

It was about half-tide. So when I hit the beach there was plenty of sand and shingle exposed. I checked the three fishermen's huts and hunted along the hundred yard stretch to the southern end of the beach, and found nothing. Just the usual junk you find on the North Sea shoreline: plastic bottles, driftwood and, paradoxically, empty halves of grapefruit from some shipboard breakfast table. They weren't supposed to dump stuff like that any more, but some ships did still.

Thankfully, there was nothing unusual in sight. I turned when I reached the rocks at the end of the beach and scanned the cliffs. Nothing up there either. No dead body hanging suspended. So far, so good.

Now I had a problem. I couldn't go north. In that direction, the cliff curved and jutted out into deep water, making it impossible to get round.

At the southern end of the bay I could scramble across rocks and get round the protruding cliff — 'Wreckers' Nab' — but I couldn't stay on the next little beach for long. There, the sea came right up to the cliff even before high water, and as the tide rose I wouldn't be able to get back here either.

To try it, or not? I stood still for a moment, bracing myself against the wind shrieking in from the sea, closing my eyes against the needle-tipped sleet, and thinking. I could see her face. She was as real to me as if she had been standing in front of me right then. I knew I had to risk it. I had to go on. I had to know if she was there or not.

Ignoring the pounding sea to my left, as well as the sheets of icy spray and the blasts of sleet, I clambered across the boulders at the southern end of the bay and reached round the small headland into the next cove. Back on firm sand, I took stock. This beach was about half a mile in length. Ten minutes to the far end, say, and ten minutes back should do it. It had better. The tide was coming in fast.

The first danger point would be a shallow depression about a hundred yards from where I was standing. That was where the water got deepest quickest. I would have to be back past that in good time. And I would have to come back because there was no other way off the beach.

Jimmy Mack had once told me there was a way but I'd never seen anything to suggest it. The shale walls were not climbable and there was no way round the headland at the far end. Deep water saw to that. Probably Jimmy's route had gone with most of the sailors' trod one day when sections of cliff slid into the sea.

I grimaced and set off, alternating between a fast walk and jogging. As I went I scanned the cliff walls and the beach ahead of me. The sand changed from firm to ultra soft, slowing me down. I ploughed on, breathing hard with the extra effort. My legs began to ache. The tension rose. This was going to take longer than I had allowed but I couldn't give up. I had to see it through.

I stopped fifty yards short of the rock wall at the far end. That was close enough. She wasn't here. Not on the beach or spread-eagled halfway down the cliffs either. Time to get back.

Quite soon after I turned round I realized I'd left it a bit late. Ahead of me I could see thin sheets of water spreading across the remaining dry sand faster than I had anticipated. I redoubled my efforts but the sand was so soft that running was impossible. Halfway back I could see that the returning tide was obliterating the footprints I had made on the outward leg. I had to move faster.

I grimaced and urged myself on. Faster! Faster!

I repeated the mantra more and more urgently, and kept on doing it. I willed my aching thighs to lift higher and press down harder.

A wave bigger than the rest suddenly streamed across the sand in front of me and washed over my boots. Another one followed, reaching up to my knees. Before I knew it, I was into the shallow depression and the water was waist-deep. I got through and kept going. Desperately, I floundered over the last fifty yards of sand and hurled myself onto the rocks, to begin the scramble round the headland.

I was up to my chest now in icy water that swirled all around me in violent spasms. Huge surges threatened to suck me out to sea as they retreated. My feet skidded on wet rock and seaweed. Spray arced over my head. I ducked my face against a shower of hail. Then a wall of water towered over me and crashed down to slam me against a big rock. I wrapped my arms around it and hung on desperately, face pressed hard against the icy, slimy surface. My feet slipped, leaving me hanging on by my arms, stretched full-length.

Mercifully, the water level subsided. But I knew it would only be for a moment. I moved on fast, threshing madly through knee-deep water. Panic was close. Another wave like the last one would do for me.

I made it. I felt shingle under my boots, and then I came out of the water and reached sand. I didn't stop. Not for a moment. I kept going, past Jimmy's boat and the little fishermens' huts, going straight for the foot of the track. I was safe from the sea but I was

43

dangerously wet and cold. I had no time to spare.

The climb back up the track took most of my remaining strength. I took risks on wet rock, and forged on. I couldn't get home fast enough.

★ ★ ★

I filled the bath, climbed in and indulged myself in a really long soak in wonderfully hot water. What I'd just done was stupid, plain stupid. It could have been fatal. Jimmy would shake his head when I told him I'd nearly been caught by the tide. His opinion of me wouldn't be enhanced. No two tides were the same, he would tell me. You couldn't depend on small margins. I hadn't allowed enough time. And for what?

I knew all that, but as well as being cold I was relieved and happy. What else could I have done? I'd had to satisfy myself that the beaches and cliff walls in at least the immediate vicinity were not occupied by my mysterious visitor, the girl who had come out of the night.

I could have called it in, I suppose. Contacted Bill Peart even. Despite the girl's plea, and her obvious fear? Well, yes. Despite that I could have done it.

But it didn't feel like the right thing to have done, and it was too late for that now anyway. At least I'd satisfied myself. She wasn't dead on the beach, and she wasn't lying somewhere nearby badly injured. I could rest more easily.

It took me a while to get warmed up. I loaded the stove with wood. Then I closed the little kitchen window. I'd had more than enough ventilation for one day. But I was more relaxed, and even content. The girl had gone. Good luck to her.

8

Bill Peart turned up again first thing the next morning. This time he came in a big posh Volvo 4 × 4 with yellow and black zig-zag patterns all over it. I went out to meet him.

I inspected the vehicle.

'What do you think?' he said.

'Nice.'

He nodded. 'We could do with a few more of these.'

'Pity about the colour scheme.'

He scowled and followed me inside.

'Coffee?'

'Yeah.'

I put the kettle on once again. My main task in life these days, it seemed.

'The chief says he's trying to get more,' Bill chuntered on, 'but every time he asks, the chairman of the Police Authority reminds him how much they cost. Mind you, he also says cracking this case could be worth a couple more of them.'

'So there's your incentive.' I grinned. 'How are you getting on with it?'

'Not great.'

That's what I had assumed. He wouldn't

have come to see me again so soon if everything had been going splendidly.

He peered at my face. 'What the hell happened to you?'

'This?' I fingered my bruises and abrasions. 'A stone wall hit me.'

He shook his head in disbelief. 'It did a good job. Maybe you're not cut out for work as a private eye?'

'Thanks, Bill. So what have you got on the bodies?'

'Forensics have come up with some info in the path lab.'

'And?'

'Two female bodies. One male.'

'Well done, them!'

He ignored my sarcasm, probably because he was used to it.

'Ages range between twenty-five and thirty-three. They also say they're all foreign.'

'Ethnic descent, you mean, or . . . ?'

He shook his head. 'Foreign. They didn't grow up here. The male is, or was, Chinese. The females are both from somewhere in Eastern Europe. Ukraine or Poland, probably.'

'How can they tell?'

'Something to do with chemicals in the body. You grow up on Teesside, you'll have bits of steel and slag in your DNA, I expect.

Grow up in China, and you have rice grains, and whatnot.'

I shook my head. 'That right?'

'Something like that. You'll have to ask the boffins, if you want to know more.'

'Boffins, eh? You still have them?'

'More than ever. What we really need, though, is more boots on the ground.' He inspected his mug and added, 'Good coffee, this.'

'Thanks. It's good to know I can do something right in your book.'

'Tch, tch! Such sensitivity.'

I thought about what Bill had just said. So they were truly exotic bodies. Not what you would normally expect to find on the beach in Port Holland. Mind you, the world is on the move as never before. Plane loads of Africans arriving every day. Plane loads of Brits off to Oz and Spain. And that's without even counting the people going on holiday. I bet if I asked him, Jimmy Mack would say it was madness. And I might even agree with him.

'Could they have come off a ship?' I asked. 'Could forensics tell you that?'

'Unlikely, I'm told. The bodies had been in the water a while. There were signs of damage from . . . ' He paused, looked up at me and winced, adding, 'I don't think I want to go fishing anywhere near Port Holland again for a while.'

'But why not off a ship?'

'That's more to do with the coastguard than forensics. The currents in the area are all wrong, apparently. Bodies dumped offshore wouldn't have come into Port Holland. They would have hit the beach a lot further south.' He shrugged. 'So they say anyway.'

Bill had been doing his homework. No wonder he looked even more shagged out than usual. Despite what he'd said for openers, he'd made a lot of progress in the past twenty-four hours. I was impressed. He had obviously persuaded various people to drop what they were doing and move this case to the top of their in-trays. Perhaps it was the lure of possible new Volvos that had done it.

'So what's your take on this now?' I asked.

He shook his head. 'Early days, Frank. Early days. I take it you know nothing more?' he added hopefully.

'Not a thing.'

Was that a lie? I wasn't sure.

'It's probably either drugs trafficking or people trafficking,' Bill added with a sigh. 'That's what I'm thinking. But we'll have to be a lot further down the road before we can say for sure.'

'Keep an open mind,' I advised. 'It doesn't have to be either of those possibilities.'

He snorted and shoved his mug across for a refill. 'OK, big detective. What else could it be?'

'I don't know. Arms trafficking?'

'That's a point. I hadn't thought of that one.' He frowned. 'Catterick's not far away, is it?'

It wasn't. Catterick, in North Yorkshire. The army's biggest base. It would be full of everything lethal you had ever heard of, and more besides.

'There was a quartermaster type there that got done for flogging Nato rifles the other year, wasn't there?' I mused, ransacking my memory banks.

'That's right.' Bill frowned. 'You've got me really worried now. I'd better have a word with my new North Yorkshire colleagues.'

He didn't add anything, and I wasn't particularly interested in pursuing the subject. It was all speculation anyway. He got up to go.

'Now you've warmed your bones and drunk all my coffee, you're hitting the road, eh?'

'That's it.' Before he left he added, 'On reflection, it's probably drugs. I'd put my money on it.'

Maybe, I thought as I watched his big machine drive away. The girl hadn't seemed like a drug addict, but you didn't have to be one to be involved in the transportation of drugs. All you had to be was greedy, or in fear of somebody. I didn't know if she was greedy or not, but the girl had certainly been terrified and desperate. That seemed a good enough qualification to me.

There remained the possibility that she had been a trafficked person, or involved in smuggling F16s or Chieftain tanks — or even not involved in events at Port Holland at all, of course. There was always that possibility, too.

But my money was on her being involved. Somehow. I was sure of it. Otherwise, we were looking at a hell of a big coincidence.

9

Just before lunch I set off for Middlesbrough. I was meeting a potential client, a Jack Picknett, who wanted me to check out his place of business. He was worried about security, apparently. So his secretary said. We were meeting in a country pub in Marton, just outside what some people used to call 'Steel City', before they stopped making the stuff there.

I arrived in the car park and sat for a few moments. I was early. So I had time to think some more about my mysterious visitor back at Risky Point, which I would have preferred not to do. She was taking over my life.

Once again, though, I got no further. I knew no more about her now than I had that first night, apart from the fact that people were looking for her. That seemed to suggest she might still be around. So when I got home I would carry on looking for her as well, just in case she hadn't got clean away. I was still worried she was supposed to be a fourth headless body.

★ ★ ★

I was meeting my potential client in the restaurant. I can't say I was particularly hungry or looking forward to a posh meal. I wasn't in the mood. But sometimes you can't afford to turn down an offer you wouldn't have made yourself. It doesn't hurt to be gracious occasionally.

I asked for the table booked in the name of 'Picknett', adding that I was a little early. The waitress took me straight to a table by a window overlooking an immaculate lawn that was occupied by a variety of bird life. The feeders dotted around indicated that the birds were part of the regular entertainment. That was OK by me. I quite liked looking at birds that for once were not seagulls.

The waitress went off to fetch me a glass of orange juice while I waited. I wouldn't have minded a beer, but first impressions can count for a lot when you're meeting a prospective new client. I wanted to learn more about the job before I risked blowing it.

'Mr Doy?'

I turned and looked up at a tall woman somewhere in her early thirties with long blonde hair who was towering over me.

'Yes?'

'Thank you for coming. I'm Ms Picknett.'

I stood up. We shook hands. Then she moved round the table to sit down opposite me, giving me time to adjust.

'Anything wrong?' she asked, picking up on my confusion.

'No, not a thing. It's very pleasant here. Jack?' I added.

'Without the 'k'.'

'Jac?'

'That's it.'

I chuckled and shook my head, trying hard to rid myself of the image of 'Jack Picknett' I had conjured up in advance: a fat, balding, middle-aged, businessman.

'It sounds much the same.'

She smiled and nodded agreement.

'Your secretary could have warned me.'

'She likes to have her little joke.'

The waitress returned with my orange juice. Jac frowned at it and invited me to share a carafe of white wine with her. How could I refuse?

'Did my secretary say anything about what I wanted?' she asked, getting down to business.

'Not really. It was just a brief conversation. She said you would like to meet me to discuss security in your business premises.'

Jac nodded. 'That's right. I own an art gallery in town. It's not exactly a salubrious area and I'm concerned about security. I would like you to check the place over and give me your advice, and an estimate of costs for an upgrade.'

Fair enough. I was a little surprised that she hadn't gone straight to one of the big security companies, or approached the issue in collaboration with her insurer, but cost might be an issue. Perhaps she couldn't afford a Rolls-Royce solution.

'I take it you're in the area designated for regeneration?' I said.

'Yes, that's right.' She smiled and added, 'You're probably thinking it's likely to be an uphill challenge, which it is, of course, but Middlesbrough needs businesses like mine. We hope to make a difference.'

My turn to nod. I couldn't disagree with any of that. I felt like wishing her luck.

'So how did you hear about me? I don't advertise my services.'

'I know Lydia. We're old friends.'

Ah! My artist ex-girlfriend. At least, I assumed she was ex. We certainly hadn't seen each other for a long while.

Jac added, 'Lydia says you're a good man. A conventional attitude towards art, but reliable and good at what you do.'

I arched my eyebrows. 'Lydia said all that? What a cheek!'

'Oh, I wouldn't worry about it,' Jac said. 'I'm a traditionalist myself when it comes to art. I like to see paint on canvas, and canvas on a wall. Lydia is different, isn't she?'

I grinned. I was beginning to like Jac Picknett.

'She calls it Performance Art.'

'Yes, I know she does. That's what it is.'

Whatever the official term for it, Lydia didn't need security alarms. The challenge lay in persuading anybody to stop and watch.

'Are we going to be able to do business together, do you think?' Jac asked, giving me an arch smile.

'Oh, yes,' I assured her. 'I'm sure we are.'

★   ★   ★

Contrary to my expectations in advance, we had a pleasant lunch. Making it even better, Jac declined my offer to pay. We discussed her security requirements and arranged for me to pay her a visit at the gallery in a few days' time. Then we parted with a handshake and a chuckle, having got on very well together.

My good mood changed abruptly when I arrived back at Risky Point to find someone had smashed the front door open. Inside, the place was a mess. Furniture overturned, cupboards emptied, broken crockery and glass all over the place. Whoever had done it

56

had gone through the entire house like a hurricane.

My mood swung from shock to anger, and then rage. Bastards! I wasn't in any doubt who was responsible. They had come back. I should have anticipated it.

I wondered if Jimmy had seen or heard anything. He should have done. Middle of the day? He couldn't have missed them.

Then I began to worry. I left the house and raced over to Jimmy's place.

The front door to his cottage must have been open. They hadn't had to smash their way through that. I went inside and saw they had saved their energy for the work ahead of them. Jimmy's place was as big a mess as mine.

Jimmy himself was on the floor in the living room. For a dreadful moment I thought the worst. Then he moved. He raised an arm. I rushed over to him.

'I'm all right,' he whispered.

'Sure you are.'

But he wasn't. His face was a mess and he wasn't moving much. He'd taken a pummelling.

'The same people?' I asked.

'The same.'

I took out my mobile and called for an emergency ambulance. Fifteen minutes, they said. I told them to try to make it faster than that.

Then I questioned Jimmy about his injuries and examined him gently, but I didn't move him or offer him painkillers. I just laid a blanket over him to try to keep him warm. It was hard to be sure but I suspected fractured ribs and an arm, as well as concussion. My biggest worry was internal damage.

I fretted while we waited. He needed to be in hospital. All I could safely do was try to keep him warm and keep him company until help arrived. I've rarely felt so useless and impotent.

The paramedics came, thank God, and did their first-responder stuff before taking Jimmy away. One of them kept up a cheerful banter to make sure he stayed conscious but none of them had much to say to me. I didn't press them with questions or interfere in any other way. They had enough to do. The last thing I wanted was to distract them.

Before they loaded Jimmy into the ambulance he rallied and indicated he wanted to speak to me. I leaned down to him.

'I told them nothing, Frank,' he whispered. 'They still haven't got her.'

'OK, Jimmy. Thanks.'

I winked, gripped his hand for a moment and then stepped back. I just wished he had known something worthwhile to tell them. He might have been spared a beating then. Probably not, though.

10

I had two new pressing problems now, in addition to the ones I had started off with. I had two houses to clear up, and I had to decide how I was going to tell Bill Peart what had happened. I was more worried about the latter.

I knew I would have to tell him. Burglary or breaking-and-entry, whatever you wanted to call it, was one thing. The assault on Jimmy Mack was in a different category altogether. If they had worked me over, I might have put up with it and gone looking for them in my own time. But the business with Jimmy was a different matter. The hospital authorities would have reported that to the police. There was no way it could be kept quiet.

While I was still mulling things over, I saw a police Volvo 4 × 4 turn off the road onto our track. Long before I could positively identify the driver I knew one of my minor problems had disappeared. I didn't have to worry any more about how to actually contact Bill Peart.

I shut the door to Jimmy's cottage and began to walk back to mine. By the time I got there, Bill had parked and got out. He stood looking at my front door. Then he turned and stared at me.

'What you been up to, Frankie boy?'

'Come on inside, Bill. It's too bloody cold out here. You can help me clear up.'

He followed me inside and whistled when he saw the state of the place. Then he got on his radio and called up some help. I was too weary and dispirited even to think of trying to stop him.

I started turning things the right way up but Bill stopped me. 'Leave it!' he said sharply. 'Leave it for forensics. Come on. I'll buy you a pint down the road. We'll just sit in the vehicle while we wait for my lads to arrive.'

I wasn't keen on the suggestion. This was my home he was talking about handing over to strangers. On the other hand, I wasn't feeling up to doing much myself, and I would just be in the way of the forensics people. Besides, I couldn't stop them going through Jimmy's place, whatever happened here. So I let it happen.

'The lads are very good,' Bill said reassuringly as we trooped out to his Volvo. 'They'll respect the place and be careful. They know you're a mate.'

I smiled ruefully and rallied. 'You don't

want to be thought a mate of mine, Bill. You might get beaten up and your front door smashed in. Anyway, how did you manage to get here so fast?'

'I was in Port Holland and I heard some chatter on the radio. When Risky Point was mentioned I thought I'd better get over here.'

'Port Holland again?'

'Again. No more bodies, though.'

'Thank God for that!'

He had dispelled my immediate fear. No more bodies. That meant they still hadn't found her.

* * *

The Smugglers, four miles down the road, wasn't a bad pub. In fact, it was very pleasant. Not that I was in the mood for frivolities. We sat in a corner of the very quiet bar and Bill bought a couple of pints.

'So what's going on?' he asked.

'Fucked if I know.'

'No idea?'

I sighed wearily and made a start.

'When I came home the other day I found two guys trying to break into my house. I stopped them. Things got a bit out of hand but Jimmy came to the rescue with his shotgun.'

'His legally held shotgun?'

'Of course.'

I certainly hoped it was.

'And it was them again?'

'So Jimmy said.'

'Boy!' Bill sighed and swigged his beer. 'Didn't even think of me? Sometimes I don't know why I bother calling you a pal.'

'You were busy with bodies on the beach,' I protested. 'You had enough to do.'

'There's a whole police force behind me.' He held his beer up to the light and squinted at it before adding, 'Maybe two, if it's serious enough.'

'I thought I could handle it. I thought I had handled it.'

'Yeah. You did. Terrific.'

'What's wrong with your beer? Got floaters in it?'

'Real ale, eh?' he said, putting his glass down.

'What's wrong with that? Anyway, I'm hungry. Do they have any crisps at the bar?'

He just looked at me. Then he carried on with what he wanted to say.

'Humour me,' he said. 'Forget I'm a cop. Just for the moment. These two tough guys? Any idea who they were?'

I shook my head. 'I'd never seen them before.'

'That's not the same thing, is it?'

'What do you want me to say, Bill? I have no more idea now than I had the other day, when they were trying to break into my house.'

He changed the subject. 'Where have you been today?'

'To see a client — a potential client. Business development.'

'Connected with this?'

I shook my head. 'She's a friend of Lydia's. She has an art gallery in Middlesbrough.'

'She?'

'Yes, she's a she.'

'Nice. And nothing to do with this?'

'I'm going to see if they have any crisps. Another pint?'

He shook his head. 'I'm on duty.'

They had only cheese and onion, which suited me well enough. I got a packet for Bill, too, hoping they wouldn't interfere with his sense of duty.

When I got back to my seat, Bill said, 'I wonder what those fellers were looking for. There must have been something, the way they turned everything over.'

'Just intent on maximum damage, probably. They got the worst of it the other day. Besides, they must have realized quite quickly there was no hidden treasure at Risky Point.'

'Really? Nothing else to help explain it?'

We seemed to have reached a crossroads. Either we continued down the road together or we went our separate ways. I didn't struggle with that for long.

'I might be able to help you a bit there,' I said carefully. It seemed time to let him in on the secret. 'They were searching for a woman. At least, I think they were.'

I didn't like the way Bill looked at me then. It was with a mixture of fury and contempt.

'Why ever would they look for a woman in your house?'

'Well, it's not what you think.'

'It never is, where you're concerned. Here I am, doing my best to try to help you, and — '

'I know, I know!' I said soothingly. 'Let me explain.'

So I told him about my nocturnal visitor.

He shook his head afterwards. 'It just gets worse,' he said bitterly. 'I've got this shitty case at Port Holland to deal with, a chief constable that wants me out of the way, and you want to complicate my life further by telling me — '

'You did ask!'

'Yeah. I did. You're right. And now I wish I hadn't.'

We talked a bit more. Bill calmed down and said he thought it was probably a coincidence, that there was no connection between my visitor and what had happened at Port Holland a few miles to the south. That's what he said, at least. I didn't argue, partly because I had no evidence to the contrary. All I had was a gut feeling. That was enough for me, but not for him.

'We'll see if we can find any prints,' Bill said in conclusion. 'See if your house was turned over by anyone we know. And we'll do the usual things. But my feeling is that they're long gone, like the woman. They won't any of them be back to Risky Point again.

'Come on,' he added. 'Let's get you back home. You've got a lot of clearing up to do.'

'If you want to stay and help,' I said hopefully, 'there might be a fish supper in it for you?'

'I've got a lot of work to do,' he said, shaking his head. 'And a home to go back to sometime.'

I could empathize with him on that. His home probably wasn't all smashed up either.

11

It took me a couple of days to clear up. My heart wasn't in it to start with, but it had to be done. Even more than my own house, I wanted to get Jimmy's place ready for when he came home. The advice that he would indeed be coming home, that he wasn't on the way out, was a relief and helped fortify my resolve. I enlisted the help of a local woman who I knew cleaned holiday cottages in the area, and between us we got it done. Well, between us and a joiner to repair my door and a man who was good at mending sash windows.

Before she left for the last time, Ellen, the cleaning lady, said, 'The two of you could probably do with someone like me on a regular basis.'

'That's an idea,' I admitted. 'I'll see what he says.'

I had a quick look round before shutting Jimmy's door and added, 'It looks better in there than I've ever seen it.'

She laughed, but she was pleased. I think she felt appreciated, which is always a good feeling to have.

'It needed a woman's touch,' I added.

'Actually,' she said, 'I wouldn't mind working here regularly. It's nearer than where I usually work.'

'Where's that?' I asked as I walked her to her car.

'Port Holland. I do cottages there, and occasionally I work at the art centre.'

'Art centre? I didn't know there was one.'

'Oh, yes. It's been there about a year. Just outside the village, actually. Meridion House? It's a big place.

'To be honest,' she added, 'I'm not so keen on going down there at the moment, with all this trouble.'

'Trouble?'

She shuddered. 'Since they started finding bodies on the beach.'

I nodded. 'It's a nasty business.'

'It is. So I've enjoyed being here for a couple of days. It's taken my mind off it all.'

I watched her drive away and gave her a last wave. Then I went inside to work out what I was going to do next.

★　★　★

The next morning I set out early to do some more searching. I hadn't forgotten my mysterious visitor. Maybe she was long gone but my head was full of unanswered questions. About dead bodies, as well as the one still alive when last seen. I needed to refresh my ideas.

I drove north to Skinningrove, where once there had been a steelworks with its own harbour for shipping coal in and pig iron and steel out. Now there was a museum and a few streets of old terraced houses. But the jetty was there still, and much prized by anglers for the cod, whiting and bass they could catch from it. There was nothing there for me, in all honesty, but Skinningrove was a geographical benchmark. Nowhere north of there, I judged, would be relevant to my searches.

I left the Land Rover down by the jetty and walked up onto the nearby cliffs to look down on Hummersea Old Harbour, where once alum shale was quarried, burned in the alum works and shipped to the textile industries. At low tide you could see two trenches in the flat expanse of shale rocks, the Hummersea Scars, where in the olden days men had hacked out channels for their boats and ships to come close inshore. From the beach you could fish now for codling and whiting, and for dab and flounder. And for mackerel in the summer. Jimmy Mack had told me. He knew a thing or two about this coast, and its fish and currents.

I travelled on to Boulby, where the four hundred foot cliffs are the highest England has to offer. Down below, just above the beach, there had once been an alum works there, too, and later iron-ore mining had taken place. All gone now, but the fish were there still, as they were to the south, in the deep, kelp-filled pools where a man brave enough to risk the tides could get a good catch of big winter cod. Jimmy had told me that, too.

Just a little further south again you got to my backyard, and then you came to Port Holland. It wasn't far. I reached it while the light was still good. The village was well-dug into the cliff, snug against the harsh wind and the threat of more sleet.

I descended a rough path to the beach and poked around for a half hour. There were a few cobles pulled up onto the shingle by the fishermen's huts. The ruined harbour, I could see, had been partially repaired in order to accommodate the magnificent pleasure craft that bobbed up and down against the repaired jetty. It was a big one. Jimmy had been right about all of this, too. Money had been spent here recently to accommodate a rich man's plaything.

I didn't stay long. By the time I had

climbed back up the cliff path, the light was fading fast and the weather was even more threatening. I drove home thoughtfully, making a point of going round by Meridion House, a mile or so out of Port Holland. The car I saw entering the ornate gateway reminded me of another car I had seen recently. The same colour, at least. Blue. I didn't have a chance to read the licence plate before it accelerated up the curving drive and out of sight behind a screen of ancient Scots pine.

★   ★   ★

Back at Risky Point I took stock. What did I have? Any new insights?

Nothing concrete, but I did have a few more thoughts and questions.

First, why would anyone wanting rid of three bodies dump them on the beach at Port Holland? There were so many better places within easy reach, places where they were unlikely to be discovered. Deep, kelp-filled pools would do the job nicely, especially when there were big, fat winter cod around.

One possibility was that they were put on the beach deliberately — with considerable effort — to serve as a punishment or a warning to local people, or a local person.

Perhaps even to one who owned a big, swanky boat?

Another possibility was that they hadn't been put there at all. They had simply ended up there.

As for my nocturnal visitor, I still didn't know for sure if she was connected to all of that. What I did have was the thought that one of the many fishermen's huts dotted and clustered around old jetties and derelict harbours wouldn't be a bad place to hide away if you were on the run. For that matter, there were plenty of cottages in Port Holland itself where she might have found refuge, perhaps with people sympathetic to her plight.

Then again, Bill Peart might well be right. In fact, he probably was. If so, she had long since departed the area. Somehow she must have. That was the most likely option when you worked through the possibilities. I just didn't believe it, not for one moment. Instinct, hunch, if you like, but if she was gone now, her presence in the first place would have been too much of a coincidence. I didn't believe in coincidence.

I got up to make myself a sandwich to tide me over until I cooked something later on, after I'd been to see Jimmy. But that didn't work out. I couldn't find the bread. A new loaf, as well. At least, I thought I'd got one out of the freezer. I must be getting delusional, I decided. Probably from living so close to Jimmy.

I shook my head, got another loaf out of the freezer and stuffed it in the microwave. What would we do without modern gadgetry? Starve, probably. Or live like Jimmy Mack. Although he seemed to manage pretty well.

While I waited for the bread to defrost, my mind went back to the car I'd seen turning into the gateway at Meridion House. The memory nagged at me. Could it have been the same one, the car that had been here a couple of days ago? Surely not? Not going into an art centre.

The make and colour were right, but there must be millions of dark blue VW saloons running around. Passat. That was the model. Hard as I tried, I couldn't think of any distinguishing feature on the tough guys' car.

Meridion House, though? I hadn't noticed a sign to say it was an art centre but Ellen wouldn't be wrong about that. She worked there, after all. They probably just hadn't got round to putting a sign up yet.

All I could recall about the place was that it had been built as the summer home for a Middlesbrough ironmaster, a place where he could let the wind blow the dust and fumes out of his lungs. In that sense, it was similar to Port Holland itself, which had been built by a Tyneside industrialist. Perhaps the two men had been buddies, as well as competitors? Ironmasters against the world!

The microwave pinged. I took the bread out and cut a couple of hefty slices. I buttered them. Then I couldn't find the cheese, the big chunk of yellow cheddar I liked so much. Instead, I had to open a tin of pork luncheon meat. Real gourmet stuff! I made a mug of tea to go with it and sat down to eat.

So Meridion House was an art centre now? Well, it made sense. Runswick Bay, not far away, was a popular spot with painters. So was Whitby, a little further south. In fact, almost anywhere on this stretch of coast was worth painting.

But an art centre? I wondered what they did there. Exhibitions? Holidays for painters? I would have to go and have a look round sometime. I'd never been.

That brought Jac Picknett to mind, and the fact that I had promised to check out her gallery. Events of the last couple of days had rather driven her out of mind. I wondered if she had heard anything about Meridion House. I'd have to ask her.

Right now, though, I needed to get over to see Jimmy Mack. Visiting him in hospital was the least I could do for him.

12

Jimmy was in James Cook University Hospital, in Middlesbrough. I felt wretchedly guilty about what had happened to him, but the sight of him relieved some of that. He was enjoying himself, and he grinned when he saw me.

'It's all right, here,' he told me straight away.

'Considering?'

'Aye, considering.' He held up the arm that was in plaster for my inspection. 'But they've been looking after me.'

'That's good. I'm really sorry, Jimmy. This shouldn't have come down on you.'

'It's all right,' he said. 'I'll see that you pay for it.'

'Endless cups of coffee?'

'At least.' He peered at me suspiciously. 'Where's my grapes? And my flowers? Don't tell me you haven't brought any?'

'Sorry, Jim,' I said helplessly.

'It doesn't matter. It's no more than I expected. Some neighbour!'

A nurse bustled up to us. 'Five minutes,' she said to me. 'Don't you go tiring him.'

Jimmy winked at me after she had left. 'See how they look after me?'

I grinned. 'I'd better get on with it, then.'

'That policeman friend of yours has been to see me.'

'Bill Peart? Has he now?'

I was surprised, and pleased.

'What did he have to say?'

'Nothing, really. He was mostly interested in asking questions, but there wasn't much I could tell him.'

'He knows what happened, by the way. After this,' I said with a shrug, 'I had to tell him.'

'About the girl, as well?'

I nodded. 'But he doesn't think she's connected to the bodies on the beach.'

'Maybe she isn't.'

'Something I was going to ask you, Jim. If you dumped something in one of them deep, kelp pools up around Boulby, somewhere like Boulby Gully, would it stay there, do you think?'

'Something like a body?' he said craftily.

I nodded.

He considered the question and said, 'Maybe not. There's strong currents all the way along the foot of the cliffs. They would probably wash it out.'

'So where would it end up?'

'Hard to say.' He frowned thoughtfully. 'On a beach, eventually, I suppose. Further south, somewhere.'

'Port Holland, maybe?'

He looked at me and nodded. 'I can't think of anywhere more likely.'

'So maybe they weren't dumped there, those three bodies. Maybe they just ended up there?'

Jimmy nodded. 'That's been my feeling all along. I mean, why would you just dump them there, where folk could see them?'

'I've been wondering that myself.'

I nodded and thought about it some more, and could find nothing wrong with the way we were both thinking.

To change the subject and make him laugh, I said, 'I nearly got caught out by the tide the other day.'

He just looked at me, his grizzled face ready to break out into laughter.

'I mean it!'

I told him what had happened. He started taking me seriously then.

'You could have got up the cliff.'

'I recalled you saying there was a way off that beach, but I couldn't see it.'

He frowned and said, 'Well, it might not be there now, I suppose. But there used to be a way.'

I thought he was probably right. Erosion would have removed whatever route he'd had in mind.

'Towards yon end,' he said slowly, 'did you notice where the sandstone comes down to the bottom?'

I shook my head. Local geology had been the last thing on my mind.

'Most of the way along it's just the shale, and that's no good. But you could get up where the sandstone is. There used to be a few iron handholds hammered into the rock. You used them in the tricky places.'

'How long ago was this, Jimmy?' I said gently.

'How long?' He frowned in thought for a moment. 'The last time I went up there, I'd have been about eleven.' His face creased with smiles and he added, 'I got merry heck off Father!'

I smiled, too. The very idea of Jimmy ever being eleven was enough to bring it out of me.

We talked for a few minutes about Jimmy's father, who seemed to have been a tough old character indeed. He'd had to be. Fishing was never an easy way to make a living.

Jimmy yawned. He was getting tired.

'Let me ask you something else, Jimmy, before I go and let you get some rest. There's a big house just outside Port Holland called Meridion House. Do you know it?'

He nodded. 'It changed hands a year or two ago. That fellow with the fancy boat bought it.'

'It's supposed to be an art centre.'

Jimmy shook his head at that. The very idea!

'Well,' he said, 'there's some funny people around. That might explain it, I suppose.'

'Funny?'

'Foreign,' he said with satisfaction, as if that really did clinch it.

'Not fishermen, you mean?'

He grinned. 'Now you're having me on!'

I laughed. 'Just a bit. Real foreign, you mean?'

'Real foreign.'

I supposed the presence of an art centre might explain that, depending on what was done at the centre.

'You don't know anything else about the place?'

He shook his head. 'Why?'

I shrugged. 'Nothing, really. It's just that when I was driving past this afternoon I saw a car the same type and colour those two thugs had. Probably just a coincidence.'

After a moment, Jimmy said, 'Did it have a rear mudflap missing, on the driver's side?'

'No idea. It was too dark. Did theirs have one missing?'

'That's just about all I do remember about it. I saw it was missing when I was lying on the ground,' he added grimly.

I hurried to change the subject.

'So how are you feeling, generally?'

'Never better.'

I was sure that was a lie, but it was a good one. I didn't mind him trying to spare my feelings.

'Well, the good news is that after two days of hard work, both our houses are just about back to normal.'

'Mended, you mean?'

I nodded. 'Mended — and cleaned. I got Ellen, that woman who does holiday cottages, to give me a hand. She's brilliant.'

'Aye. She is.'

He was quiet for a little while. Remembering what the nurse had said, I wondered if I was over-taxing him.

Then he turned to me and said, 'Thank you, Frank. I can't wait to get back home.'

I could swear there was a tear in his eye. I touched his good arm gently and left.

★   ★   ★

On the way out, the same nurse I had seen before bustled up to me.

'How did you find Mr Mack?'

I smiled. 'He seems pretty good to me. You've done really well for him.'

She smiled. 'Another couple of days and he'll be ready to go home.'

'I don't think he'll want to.'

She laughed. 'Oh, he will! I'm sure of that.'

'No lasting damage?'

'No. He'll be fine.'

'That's a relief. Thank you again.'

As I walked over to the Land Rover, I was thinking that Jimmy might be fine, but I knew two miserable creatures who would not be when I caught up with them. Cretins! And I would do that — I would find them. Payback time couldn't come soon enough.

13

The phone rang soon after I got back in the house. It was Bill Peart.

'You're lucky,' I told him. 'I've just got in. Did you try my mobile?'

'It costs money to ring mobiles.'

'There is that,' I said, raising my eyebrows. 'What can I do for you?'

'I've been thinking about the bodies at Port Holland.'

Day and night, it seemed. Not too surprising, really. He would feel he had responsibility for them.

'And?'

'Well . . . ' He was struggling. 'Can you think of any reason for them being naked?'

'A couple, actually,' I said with a smile.

He made a disgusted noise and said, 'Seriously.'

'Yes, even seriously.'

'Go on.'

'It reduces the possibility of identification even further.'

'Yeah. Got that. Anything else?'

I'd been thinking of this during my long walk along the cliffs. Now I wondered if Bill had got to the same place as me.

'It would be easier to get victims to take their own clothes off than to do it for them when they're dead.'

'That's what I thought,' he said with a big sigh. After a moment's silence he added, 'You know what this means for the girl that came to your house, don't you?'

'Yes. She was meant to be a victim, as well.'

'Exactly. So she was involved.'

What he didn't say, but I knew as well as he did, was that she was lucky she'd got away — and how had she managed that?

'I wonder what happened to her?' Bill said reflectively.

'That's been tormenting me, as well,' I told him before I hung up.

★   ★   ★

I was hungry by then, but I couldn't lay my hands on anything I wanted. I was too distracted. What the hell did Bill think — I was his private, unpaid consultant?

The situation was getting to me. It was all right for him but I had a living to make, and I was struggling. I was neglecting simple things, and forgetting others. Imagining things, as well. No defrosted bread again! And where the hell was the packet of sausages

I bought yesterday? I couldn't find my favourite coffee mug either. Shit!

At least I had plenty of wine and beer. There was nutrition in that, wasn't there, I thought wearily, as I settled in a chair with a bottle of Caledonian 80 and an opener.

Enough, anyway. Enough nutrition to last me until I got into Middlesbrough tomorrow. That was when I was due to visit Jac Picknett and check out her gallery before I advised her on security arrangements. Getting back to my day job. And doing some shopping while I was at it.

I yawned as I chomped my way through a bag of crisps, not having found anything else that took my fancy and was as easy to prepare. It had been a long day, and an unsatisfactory one. Nothing resolved. But at least Jimmy was on the mend. We were getting back to normal. I should concentrate on a positive like that, and put aside the stuff I couldn't do anything about.

★ ★ ★

Then the phone rang again. I picked it up.

'Doy? Frank Doy?'

'Yes?'

'How did you like your house when we were finished with it?'

That was followed by a mad laugh. Before I could reply, the voice said, 'Keep out of things that are nothing to do with you. Next time you won't have a house to go back to — or a neighbour either.'

'Fuck you!'

That was the best I could manage. The phone went dead. I scowled at it. Nice!

Perversely, though, on reflection I was almost pleased. It meant they were still around, and it meant that for some reason I worried them. They were going to be a hell of a lot more worried when I caught up with them.

I got up and did the rounds, checking doors and windows, before I went to bed. Second nature. Old habits. The small window in the kitchen was not properly shut. A slim wedge of cardboard that I must have jammed in to stop it rattling was the reason. I left it. If the wind got up again I would regret taking it out.

That was it. Everything was back to normal. More or less. Well, that was one way of looking at it.

14

Especially after that phone call, I couldn't get the blue car out of my mind. I had seen such a car entering the grounds of the art centre, but was it the one with the missing mudflap?

There was only one place to start looking, if I was going to find out. So the next morning I set off for Meridion House soon after breakfast. First, I had to scrape ice off the windscreen. The weather had changed. It was a lot colder now but the wind had died down, the rain and sleet had stopped and it was a pleasantly bright day.

The entrance to the Meridion House estate was very grand. You drove between two huge sandstone pillars and beneath a wrought-iron arch that spanned them. Then you followed a drive that wound its way through a patch of stunted and distorted Scots pine that must have been planted when the house was built. No doubt the original idea was to have elegant mature trees lining the drive, but it hadn't worked out. The wind off the North Sea had seen to that.

It was a short drive. Just a couple of hundred yards. When I rounded the final bend I came to a little hut and a barrier that would go up and down when the man in the hut at the side of the road pressed a button. I was surprised. You couldn't see any of this from the road. Now I was alerted, I glanced to either side and saw a two-foot high fence of heavy-duty timber piling that would stop anything but a main battle tank. I guessed it ran all the way around the house and its immediate environs. I was impressed. Nobody was going to force their way in here.

I stopped and wound my window down. The gatekeeper came out to see me.

'Good morning!' I said brightly.

'Good morning, sir. Do you have business here?'

'I do, yes. Frank Doy. I live at Risky Point.'

He gave me a cool, alert look. 'I don't believe you've been here before?'

'No, that's right. I haven't.'

'Are we expecting you, Mr Doy?'

'No. I don't have an appointment.'

'Then I can't admit you. Sorry.'

'You can't admit me?' I frowned at him. 'This is an art centre, isn't it?'

'It is. But it's not open to the public.'

'A private art centre? I see. Who's the owner?'

'I'm not at liberty to say.'

'Do you have any information about the

place, and what it has to offer?'

'I'm afraid not.'

This was becoming bizarre. What kind of art centre was it? OK. One last try.

'Perhaps you can tell me how I can find information — and how to get an appointment?'

'If you phone this number,' he said, pulling a business card from his pocket, 'I'm sure someone will be able to help you.'

'There's no one here at the moment who could help me?'

'I'm afraid not, no.'

I smiled sceptically and shook my head. Then I began a three-point turn, while he stood and watched. Once again, I thought, impressive security.

★ ★ ★

Back on the main road, I stopped in an unofficial lay-by from where I could watch the entrance to Meridion House. I switched off the engine and prepared to wait.

I was surprised and a little confused by my reception. It didn't seem right. I'd never heard of a *secret* art centre!

I studied the business card the gatekeeper had given me: 'Meridion House Art Centre'. There was a phone number and small print said they provided training for young artists. So, an art college? A private one? Very private, it seemed.

The card told me nothing else. The minimal information provided was, perhaps, intended simply to stop people wondering what Meridion House was. Again, I thought, quite clever. If there had been no information at all, public curiosity might have been unbounded.

I wondered if young artists needed quite so much security and privacy, but I didn't get very far with that one. Perhaps the youngsters were all from countries where people like themselves lived in golden palaces behind high walls that kept out the great unwashed. That would fit in with Jimmy Mack's oblique reference to foreigners.

I shrugged, and waited.

I waited the best part of an hour. Nobody came in or out in that time, and it was cold. I was cold. Running the engine for a few minutes every once in a while didn't do much to warm me up. I gave it up as a bad job and quit.

★   ★   ★

While I was in the vicinity, I drove into Port Holland, parked and set off to look around once more. The village itself wasn't much. Just a few terraced streets of modest cottages built originally for the workers and their families. The fine boat tied up at the jetty was the star. And pretty incongruous it looked. As I studied it, a couple of men came from below deck and began sweeping and polishing.

On such a cold, sunny morning the North Sea actually looked blue, and dangerously inviting. I made my way down the rough path to the beach, and thought once more what a mess it all was. It was a working beach, not one for holiday-makers. Broken concrete. Piles of washed-up kelp. Patches of sand and shingle. Swathes of big boulders. A few cobles, the property of men who still fished. A dozen or more fishermen's huts, most improvised from spare parts and rubbish, and collectively looking as unsightly as any scrapyard.

I couldn't help wondering if a man with a boat as big and fine as the one at the jetty couldn't have found a more decorous environment. It was handy for his house, I supposed, but still . . .   Millionaires, or billionaires, often had both yachts and houses in beautiful places, not junkyards. What was wrong with Palma or Montenegro? Either would be perfect for a private art centre, as well as for a boat like this one. Perhaps the man just liked ugly.

Still, the huts caught your eye. They were interesting. I wandered between them. Some had windows and some had mere openings, but in both cases wooden shutters, proof against the weather, prevented anyone looking inside. Not that I needed to look inside. I knew some were storage sheds for nets and lobster pots, and for spare parts and tools for the tractors and boat engines. Others could be stayed in overnight, or for a day or two. Some of the latter would be well equipped, while others would just be empty spaces and bare floors. Fishermen were like everyone else. Not all of them would want a home from home.

A little way above the beach was the blocked-up entrance to the tunnel that was the reason for the jetty in the first place. It was built for the shipment of iron ore brought from a nineteenth-century mine some four miles inland.

There were other tunnels in the cliffs along this coast, some to facilitate the extraction of ironstone and others from the days when alum shale was mined. For over two hundred years the production of alum for textiles had been a major industry in Cleveland, and the spoil heaps you could still see in a number of places were their legacy.

As my eyes ranged along the cliff face, they picked out another tunnel entrance, one I hadn't noticed or known about before. This one seemed to be in use, judging by the well-kept, heavy-duty steel door that covered it.

I spoke about it to a man who was walking his dog along the beach.

'Yes, it's an old tunnel,' he agreed, 'but I couldn't tell you what it was for. We never knew it was there till this lot uncovered it, and claimed it. Bloody Russians!' He nodded at the boat alongside the jetty.

'Is that what they are? Russians?'

'The bloke that owns the boat, *Meridion*, is. He bought Meridion House, as well. God knows what he wants with it. It's a mouldy old dump.'

'What do they use the tunnel for?'

'It's just a storage shed, apparently. They keep spare gear for the boat there. So they say, anyway. I haven't seen inside, myself.'

'Does the tunnel go anywhere?'

'It must have done at one time. That's quality stonework around the entrance. It won't go anywhere now, though. Either it'll have been filled in or, more likely, it will have collapsed.'

I nodded and let him go on his way. He

92

was probably right — about everything. On the other hand, he might not be. If he'd told me the tunnel led to Meridion House I wouldn't have been astonished.

I wondered if Bill Peart knew about all this. It didn't take a lot of imagination to think coming into possession of an old tunnel leading down to a jetty could be useful to all sorts of people. It could even explain why someone with an oligarch's boat and an art centre had bought into a dump like this.

I turned to watch some new activity on the jetty. Newcomers were loading heavy items onto the boat. The rear end had opened up like a car ferry, and they were rolling their stuff inside on trolleys. Very simple and easy. I wondered what the cargo was, but from a distance the wooden crates gave nothing away.

I glanced at my watch and realized time was running out on me. I had less than an hour to get to Middlesbrough for my appointment with Jac Picknett. I'd better get back to the house first.

* * *

Bill Peart was still on my mind. As I was debating whether to phone him before I set off, the man himself arrived.

'If you want coffee,' I told him, 'we'll have to be quick. I'm on my way out.'

'Suits me,' he said stiffly. 'I'm a busy man.'

I switched the kettle on, reached for the mugs and said over my shoulder, 'Have you heard of a place called Meridion House?'

He shook his head.

'A mile or so outside Port Holland? That's where I've been this morning.'

He looked up, a calculating look in his eye. 'Why is that, I wonder?'

I ignored his sad attempt at clever humour.

'It's a strange place, and a bit of a mystery. Supposed to be an art centre. Owned by some Russian. At least, I was told that's what he is. He's the guy with the big boat in Port Holland, as well.'

'The *Meridion*?'

I nodded.

'Another one with more money than sense. He should have bought a football club, like the rest of them.'

'You've been talking to Jimmy Mack,' I said with a grin. 'I don't know if you're aware of this, Bill, but there's a lot of old tunnels along this coast. They date back to the days of mining.'

'That right?'

'I've been having a look around the beach at Port Holland. There's a couple there — one I knew about. It connected to the Old Park ironstone mine. It's blocked off now, of course.

'But I saw one today I wasn't aware of. It's in use, as well. The guy that owns the big boat has had it uncovered, and he uses it as a sort of boat shed. So I'm told. Might be worth looking into?'

'Why ever would I want to do that?'

'Big house, tunnels, a Russian with a big boat? It's not hard to imagine all sorts of reasons.'

Bill chuckled. 'You want me to see what I can find out?'

'It might be an idea. It's an unusual situation.'

'Aye, well.' He yawned and stretched. 'Let's solve these murders first.'

I made no further comment. Let him work it out for himself.

Bill finished his coffee quickly and got up to leave. 'Nothing more from your side?' he asked.

'Nothing.'

Just Meridion House. I'd already mentioned that. It might be something, or it might be nothing, but my mind was easier knowing that Bill had it on his to-do list. It would be less difficult for him to look into than it would be for me. Besides, I couldn't do everything. It was time he did some digging himself.

15

I found The Cleveland Contemporary Art Gallery with a few minutes to spare. It was in an old building, once the offices for a trolley bus depot. The conversion, presumably by Jac Picknett, wouldn't have been cheap. Perhaps that was why she couldn't afford top-of-the-range security and had come to see me instead.

I walked round the outside first, sizing up the job. I began by assuming the existing security was next-to-nothing. There was a lot of glass in the revamped building and I wondered if any of it was extra special. It didn't look it. Just toughened glass, with window locks a child of ten could break. Maybe a child of eight, given that we were in the centre of Middlesbrough.

The interior was pleasant enough, and suitably atmospheric. It looked, in fact, like my idea of an art gallery. Plain walls with lights illuminating a handful of paintings. Plush red carpet. A man in uniform who opened the door for me. A smart-looking young woman behind a big reception desk. A couple of possible clients, or more likely window shoppers, eyeing a small bronze of a skating woman in Victorian garb, long skirt and coat flowing behind her as she held on to a bonnet with one hand.

'Yes, Mr Doy,' the receptionist said with a welcoming smile. 'Ms Picknett is expecting you. George will show you the way.'

She beckoned the doorman, who seemed glad to have something different to do. He nodded, gave me a quick smile and gravely led the way down a corridor and up some stairs.

Jac greeted me in a friendly, if rather formal, way. She even seemed pleased to see me.

'Mr Doy,' she said, rising from behind her desk. 'How good of you to come.'

'We did arrange to meet.' I glanced at my watch. 'At this time, too.'

'Yes, of course we did. I was expecting you. Would you like coffee?'

'Later, if you don't mind. I'd prefer to make a start.'

'Of course. How would it be if I gave you a quick whistle-stop tour? It won't take long. Then I can leave you to do what you need to do.'

'Sounds good. It's Frank, by the way,' I said with a smile.

She inclined her head graciously. 'Frank.'

'And it's good to see you again. Did I say that already?'

'I don't think you did, no. But thank you. I feel the same way.'

So we were off to a good start. That's always promising with a new client. It saves a lot of hassle.

The tour didn't take long. She was right about that. The gallery was a nice place, but small. How could it be anything else without some mega corporation behind it?

'Mostly, we show paintings by modestly known artists that we know will sell,' Jac began as we set off down a long, narrow room that had once probably been a corridor. 'We are a business, after all,' she added.

I nodded. Then I paused to look at a nice watercolour of a stretch of the Cleveland coast.

'That's not far from where I live,' I told her.

'Really? Lucky you!'

She smiled a melting smile that endeared her to me, and turned away again. I happily followed her long, straight back as she smoothed her way gracefully across the carpet. It was then that I realized how extraordinarily slim she was. I could have circled the waistband of her black skirt with my hands. Not the white blouse above, though; she was well built in that way.

We moved on to enter a larger room that was given over to seascapes in oil.

'We do well with these, too,' she said. 'The Northeast is still a sea-faring region at heart.'

'Gifts for retired master mariners?'

She laughed. 'Probably. Or modern yachting enthusiasts. Whereabouts on the coast do you live, by the way?'

I told her.

'Nice,' she said, shaking her head judiciously. 'Rather wild?'

'Oh, yes. You have to hold on to your hat most days.'

She seemed to like that, as well.

We entered a large room that did its best to knock you out. I stared with surprise at the extravagantly lurid canvases that dominated all the walls. Vivid yellows, empowering pinks, raging reds, and malestrom blues. That just about summed it up.

'Your acrylics section?' I suggested.

Jac laughed again. 'It seems that way, doesn't it? These are all by young local artists from the college. I like to showcase some of their work.'

'And is this what young artists like to do these days?'

'Those that like to paint at all seem to, at the moment. Those, that is, who are not busy creating sensory experiences in other media, or trying to shock us all with political comment.'

'Well, that's enough for me. I forgot to bring my sunglasses.'

I wondered if she would laugh again, and she did. It was a soft, tinkling sound that was a sensory experience in its own right.

'I'll leave you to it, then,' she said. 'Come and rejoin me when you're through. We'll have that coffee — if you have time?'

Oh, yes. I was sure I would have the time. Apart from anything else, I was getting to like Jac Picknett more every minute I spent with her.

★ ★ ★

It didn't take me long to work out, on a rough basis, a reasonable package for the gallery. It wasn't the Tate or the Louvre, after all. Jac didn't need, and probably couldn't afford, state-of-the-art security. She just wanted a sensible package. I could set that up for her.

The package would include well-positioned CCTV cameras and monitors, good locks on internal as well as external doors, internal sensors and alarms and a lot of common-sense precautions that experience had demonstrated were as effective as anything.

'What's the damage?' Jac asked when I returned to her office.

I told her in ballpark terms.

'That's a lot better than I feared. Are you sure?'

'Security is always a compromise,' I told her. 'The more you have, the more you pay, but it's never absolute anyway. A good man — or a bad one — can always break through, given enough time and determination.

'Besides, you have to consider what kind of a place you want here. You're not trying to keep people out. You want the gallery to be welcoming and attractive to people, presumably, not a Fort Knox designed to stop anyone getting inside. What I'm proposing should be more than enough for what you have here. Have you had any problems, by the way?'

'Nothing serious — yet.'

'Let's keep it that way. I'll do some detailed costing and come back to you with my ideas. Then, if you're still interested, I'll get the hardware and software ordered. I think you should tag items with sensors that will alert someone if they are touched or moved. Meantime, there are some simple things that you can do yourself.'

'Oh? Like what?'

'Well, for one, I'd like you to make sure you're happy about everyone who works here. A lot of the thefts that do occur from art galleries involve insider assistance. Let's try and rule that out.

'Then I'd like you to think about how you organize your exhibitions and displays a bit more. Your most valuable items should be in the safest part of the gallery, or the part hardest to reach. Don't have them where someone can break a window, reach through and grab them.

'There's also some practical things worth doing on the outside of the building. You have unprotected glass on the roof. We need either to encase it or to fit bars, so someone can't just shin up a drainpipe, tap the glass out and let themselves in the easy way.

'External windows need protecting for the same reason. And outside the entrance you need some sort of impediment to stop someone crashing a stolen vehicle through the doors. Bollards, or something similar, would do it. Decorative street furniture, perhaps? A sculpture or two?'

She was looking doubtful.

'Jac, big museums have had priceless artefacts stolen in less than a minute by people who have smashed a window, climbed in and helped themselves and been away again before the alarms have got into their stride. You can't depend totally on alarms and motion sensors, or any other kind of electronic device.'

'I suppose . . . ' she started, 'but what . . . ?'

'I know an architect who would be glad to advise you on a sensitive approach to fitting these kinds of things. He's good. It's not hi-tech,' I added, 'but it can be better than that — more effective.'

She smiled at last. 'OK, Frank. That makes sense.'

'He lives in York. Mostly he protects medieval windows. I'll contact him for you, if you like?'

'Thank you, Frank. I would appreciate it. Gosh!' she added. 'There's more to this than I thought.'

'A lot of it's just common sense, and experience. You could skip the electronics altogether and still make the place a lot more secure than it currently is.'

'No,' she said firmly. 'I'm happy with what you've told me. Let's do what you're suggesting.'

'Good. I don't think you'll regret it.' I stirred my coffee. 'It's a very nice gallery, by the way. How long have you been going?'

'A year. A little more.' She shrugged. 'We're

not pulling up trees yet, but we're doing OK. Better than I expected, the truth be told.'

I nodded. 'You seem to employ a few people?'

'More than you might think, actually.' She smiled. 'Probably like you?'

'I don't employ anyone.'

'No one at all?'

'No. Not one. That suits me best. No one to argue with, that way.'

'Is that what you do — argue a lot?'

I grinned. 'So people say. Ask Lydia.'

'Maybe I will.' She threw back her head and laughed, exposing a milk-white throat that I felt a sudden urge to lick. 'But you don't seem the aggressively argumentative type to me,' she added.

'No. I'm a real softy.'

Somehow I had amused her. I could tell. I felt pleased with myself.

'How did you get into the gallery business?'

She shrugged. 'I've always been involved with the visual arts. School, college, etcetera. I liked painting. I still do. But I took stock and decided I was never going to make a decent living out of my pictures. This was a way of keeping in touch. I like what I do here anyway. I discovered a flair for business I hadn't realized I had.'

If this was all hers, she probably did have a

flair. She had done well here.

'How about you?' she added.

'Oh, it's a long story,' I said, draining my cup and making moves to be on my way.

'Too long for now?' she asked archly.

I nodded.

'Some other time, perhaps?'

'Some other time,' I agreed with a smile as I stood up.

'Oh, by the way, Jac, there's an art centre opened recently not far from where I live. Meridion House, just outside Port Holland. You haven't heard of it, have you?'

She thought for a moment and shook her head. 'What do they do?'

'No idea. I can't find anything about it. When I turned up this morning, the gatekeeper wouldn't let me in. He wouldn't tell me anything about it either.'

She frowned. 'Perhaps they're not up and running yet?'

'They've been going a year, apparently, like you.'

'It sounds an odd sort of place.' She shrugged. 'I'll see what I can find out. It's always good to know what's happening in the region.'

As I made my way out, I saw a little knot of young people who had wandered in off the street and were excitedly discussing a

106

painting. I smiled. This was a very different place altogether to Meridion House.

Back outside, I looked up and saw Jac standing at the window of her office. She gave me a wave and I waved back. I found myself looking forward to seeing her again.

16

I was drawn back to the beach at Port Holland. It was hard to say why exactly. Just a feeling that important things might happen there. Probably the boat was at the heart of my wondering. It was so big and improbable a vessel to find in that particular place. The only other boats to call Port Holland home these days were a few fishing cobles, good enough in their own way but nothing compared with *Meridion*.

From the beach *Meridion* looked big, but from the start of the jetty it seemed enormous, a real oligarch's yacht. I wouldn't have been surprised to learn it was one of those with its own submarine and helicopter. Probably a missile battery, as well, in case the mackerel started attacking in numbers.

'What do you want?'

I turned. Three men were walking towards me. Crew members, I assumed. They were dressed alike, in navy trousers and sweaters, and padded jackets.

'I don't want anything,' I told the spokesman. 'Just having a look round.'

Unsmiling, he stared hard at me and said,

'Get off the jetty. We've got work to do.'

'I wasn't aware this was private property.'

'Get off — now!'

They were a tough-looking trio, and more than I could handle. I took out my mobile and started punching in numbers.

'I'm calling the police,' I said mildly. 'My friends there will be interested to hear that someone in a public place is being threatened by gentlemen from a foreign-owned yacht.'

I paused, my thumb over the call button. 'What's it to be, fellas? You want me to take this further?'

'By the time they get here,' the spokesman said, 'there won't be much left of you to find.'

'I'm prepared to take the risk.'

Staring hard back at him, I pressed 'Call'.

He couldn't handle that. He glowered at me and beckoned to the others. They all walked past, heading for the boat.

'Don't get in the way!' he snapped over his shoulder.

I pressed 'End'. My answerphone back at Risky Point had just recorded another blank.

Nice people, I thought. Why would the owner of a big, posh boat want crew like that? It wasn't as if this was the Somali coast.

* * *

The encounter had intrigued me. I didn't stay on the jetty much longer, but I didn't leave Port Holland either. I climbed back up the cliff and settled down to wait and watch for a while. I wondered what work was planned for the jetty, or for the boat. Whatever it was, there didn't seem to be any hurry about it. Nothing happened for an hour or so.

By then, I was pretty well frozen and about ready to give up. I was feeling despondent, as well, having wasted some of the few hours of good daylight available in mid-November. If the guys on the jetty hadn't been so threatening I would have left long since, I told myself. Probably I wouldn't even have stayed at all. I had better things to do than this.

Then a burst of activity aboard *Meridion* changed all that and made me forget my discomfort. The rear flap I had seen in action before opened and three crew members emerged from the interior of the boat. They walked briskly along the jetty and up across the sand and shingle to join a couple more men in the same uniform who seemed to have emerged from the tunnel.

Interesting. Something was happening at last. I could hardly wait!

There was a bit of to-ing and fro-ing around the entrance to the tunnel. A couple of men laid boards across the sand, and then several trolleys bearing big wooden crates were wheeled across them.

Once on the jetty, the trolleys were rolled quickly along to the boat, across a ramp and into the cavernous interior.

I counted six crates, each about ten feet long and four high and wide. Once aboard, the big flap swung slowly shut again. Some of the crew stayed on board. The others returned along the jetty with the empty trolleys, and headed back up towards the tunnel. I watched until the door at the entrance swung shut, with them inside.

I felt vindicated. There was no way that tunnel was just a storage shed.

As for the crates . . . Well, what did you put in big wooden crates that you then put on a big, fancy boat, and all this in a ruined harbour on the North Yorkshire coast? I had my suspicions, but they were bordering on fantasy. Perhaps I wouldn't have had them at all if I hadn't been challenged so threateningly on the jetty.

★   ★   ★

That was Bill Peart's opinion as well.

'Loading stuff in broad daylight that they took from their own property and placed on their own boat?' he said. 'What's wrong with that?'

I sighed. 'You weren't there. You weren't threatened. In a public place, as well.'

'Do you want to make a formal complaint?'

'No. Not yet, anyway.'

'Well, then. They've rebuilt the jetty with their own money, as I understand it. And with an expensive boat like that, they've got to be security conscious. Besides, you're a suspicious-looking character.'

'Thanks, Bill.'

I thought hard about what I'd seen. 'There were no markings on the crates.'

'So?'

'They looked new. Well made, too. They must have had something heavy in them, all those guys to push them. And valuable.'

Bill shrugged. His complacent silence was getting on my nerves.

'There's no road down to the beach there, Bill. Whatever the crates were holding, they came out of that bloody tunnel.'

He swigged the last of his coffee and held out the mug for a refill.

'Get it yourself!'

He did. Then he stood over me, lording it, and suddenly I knew. I stared at him. He shrugged.

'You know what they're doing, don't you?'

He nodded.

'What?'

'I can't tell you. If I did, I'd have to — '

'Don't bother with the rest,' I snorted. 'And if you think you can just come here when you're cold and wet, and drink my coffee, you can — '

'National security,' he said sharply, cutting me off. 'That's all I can tell you.'

I stared at him. 'You're kidding?'

He shook his head. 'I wish I was. I've been warned off.'

'Warned off what?'

'Can't tell you.'

'What about the bodies? Are you warned off them, as well?'

'No. The case goes on. But it's nothing to do with Meridion House. I've been told.'

'And you can accept that?'

'I've got a pension to consider. The payment start date is coming up fast.'

'I hope I'm never as old as you,' I said bitterly.

'There's no chance of that, the way you're going on.'

Then he left.

17

At half-tide I went down the cliff path near my place again. There were three fishermen's huts at the bottom, on our little beach. One was Jimmy's main storage place, where he kept nets and tools, and various paraphernalia he needed for the boat. Not that he went there much these days, and even then only when the sun was shining.

A second hut was also Jimmy's, by inheritance. It had belonged to his uncle but it wasn't up to much now, and it got used even less than his main hut. The third hut wasn't much better. It belonged to a fisherman even older than Jimmy, and in the past year or two arthritis and other maladies had kept him away so long you could say it was disused. Increasingly, Jimmy's main hut was heading in the same direction. The path down to the beach was a young man's path.

There were no locks on any of the hut doors; they weren't needed. Probably there were only three or four people in the entire world who even knew the huts existed. I had a look inside them.

Only Jimmy's was what you might call

habitable, and even then it was marginal. It did have a bunk bed for occasional use, but there wasn't any bedding there now. It also had a chair and a pot-bellied, cast-iron stove in which you could burn driftwood and anything else you could find. You could make toast on it, as well. Or roast potatoes and fish. Jimmy and I had done that together a few times, while we waited for the tide or dried off and recovered from our exertions.

The hut was seldom used now, but the stove had been lit in the recent past and there were still breadcrumbs on the little table that the local mice had somehow missed. Perhaps the mice had gone away, emigrated, despairing of huts so long disused. I closed the door carefully and wedged it shut. Then I began the long climb back up the cliff.

★　★　★

The answerphone was flashing when I got back to the house. I pressed the play button.

The message was from a Mr Borovsky, who claimed to be the owner of the Meridion House Art Centre. His accent was obviously foreign, but he was nevertheless an articulate English speaker.

He said he understood that I had paid the centre a visit and been turned back. He was sorry about that. He had not been at home when I called.

The centre was not open to the public. However, he was anxious to cultivate good relations with the local community and he would be happy to meet me and show me around, if I was still interested. Ten o'clock tomorrow would be perfect from his point of view. He would be sure to be home then.

That rather pulled the rug out from beneath me. National security? What on earth had Bill Peart been talking about? There couldn't be much mystery about the place if the owner was prepared to go to this much trouble. As Groucho Marx might have said: Was it somewhere worth visiting now that I had an invitation?

For the next hour I got on with the job of ordering the equipment I needed for Jac Picknett's art gallery. I also left a message for my architect friend in York. It was a relief to have something tangible to think about and to do.

But then I came back to the girl, and the agonizing question of whether she was still alive or not. What had happened to her after she'd left here? The uncertainty and my fears for her were wearing me down.

Then the thought of the men in the blue Volkswagen Passat, and how I had seen such a car passing through the gateway to Meridion House, came to mind. I knew I had to go there, if only to rule that car out. Tomorrow, then. Tomorrow at ten.

Right now, though, I had to get to Middlesbrough to bring Mr Mack back home.

★ ★ ★

As I might have anticipated, Jimmy wasn't in the most pleasant and cooperative of moods. He had been cooped up too long.

'What kept you?' he demanded as soon as I walked through the door. 'I've been sitting here waiting.'

I glanced at my watch. I was late, it was true. Five minutes late.

I made an offering. 'The traffic, Jim. It was very heavy.'

He scowled and shuffled to his feet. A passing nurse raised her eyebrows. I picked up his bag.

'I thought you liked it here,' I said mildly.

'Liked it?' He snorted with derision. 'You stay here a few days, and see how you like it.'

'Now, now, Mr Mack!' the nurse called across the ward. 'Don't you be giving us a bad name.'

'I'll see he doesn't,' I assured her.

She grinned and waved us off.

'Sounds like you've overstayed your welcome,' I suggested.

'Them nurses! They think they're God Almighty.'

'So you've met your match?'

He didn't say anything else until we were in the Land Rover, the miserable old bugger. Then he said, 'Found that girl yet?'

'Nope.'

'Thought as much. She still around?'

'How the hell do I know? I haven't seen her. That's all I know.'

For the first time, Jimmy smiled. Then he nodded as I started the engine. 'You can always tell,' he said mysteriously.

'You can, eh? And how do I do that?'

'Missing any food?' he asked. 'Anything you thought you had, and now you find you don't?'

For a moment it didn't click. Then I shook my head, chuckled and glanced at him with admiration. 'You cunning old sod!'

★ ★ ★

I got him settled in his own place and left him to it. He could manage, and he wanted to be alone. That was what I wanted by then, too: Jimmy Mack left alone. Also, I wanted to see if I was missing any more food.

18

A loaf of bread had gone. I'd had two in the freezer. Now I had one. Possibly a pack of cheddar cheese, as well — I wasn't certain I hadn't eaten it. A bag of Brazil nuts had disappeared, and a bag of sultanas. Those I was sure about. They had been where I kept my cereal packets, alongside the muesli. My stock of tins seemed to be down a bit, as well. Sardines mostly, I thought. Other things, too. Something here; something there. Not a lot — but enough.

I checked around the house and smiled with satisfaction when I looked at the little kitchen window. The wedge of cardboard that stopped the window catch closing fully was still there, but its position was not the same. Someone had moved it, and it hadn't been me. Now I thought about it, it probably hadn't been me who had put it there in the first place. I couldn't recall that window rattling much.

So I made a cup of coffee, and sat and thought. Only food had been taken, and not much of it. Probably a bottle or two of water, as well, if I checked. Survival essentials.

I smiled happily. She was alive!

I walked over to Jimmy's place to see if he was all right and to tell him the good news. The cottage was in darkness. He'd obviously taken himself off to an early bed. I smiled and retreated. My news could wait until the morning.

The message recorder was flashing when I opened my front door. Again! I shook my head and pressed the button.

'Jac Picknett here, Frank. Would you mind giving me a call when it's convenient?'

I wondered what this was about, and hoped I hadn't lost her business. Maybe the locals had decided to pre-empt the planned new security system? With a sigh I picked up the phone.

★ ★ ★

'Hello, Frank. I'm sorry to have called you so late.'

'That's all right. It's not my bedtime yet.'

I heard her smile.

'So what's happened, Jac? A break-in?'

'No, no! Nothing like that. I just thought I would let you know I can't find anything at all about the Meridion House Art Centre.'

I began to relax.

'It's peculiar. Especially if they've been there a year, or so. Whatever they do, they need publicity. At the very least, surely they need to let the world know they're up and running? But I can't find any mention of them at all in any of the catalogues, or on the net either.'

'Maybe they're not a business?' I suggested.

She chuckled. 'Well, if they're not open to the public and they're not a business, what are they? Why would they call themselves an art centre?'

It was a good question, one that had me flummoxed as well.

'Is that why you rang?' I asked. 'To tell me that?'

'Yes.' She paused and then said, 'I'm sorry. I thought you would want to know.'

'I was worried to death! I thought you were ringing to say your gallery had been broken into, and all your paintings had been nicked.'

She laughed.

'Actually,' I added, 'this is good timing. While I was out this evening someone who says he owns Meridion House, a Mr Borovsky, rang up and left a message. He reiterated that it's not open to the public, but in the interests of good relations with his neighbours he's invited me to go and see him in the morning. He'll show me around.'

'Oh? How interesting.'

'Isn't it? I thought I would take him up on it. Do you fancy coming with me? And casting an expert eye over things?'

'Me?' She thought for a moment and then said, 'I'd love to. What time?'

I told her.

It was settled.

Afterwards, I smiled with satisfaction. It could be useful to have an expert alongside me. Besides, I had been looking forward to seeing Jac Picknett again, and I didn't mind at all if it was sooner than I had expected.

19

Jac arrived at Risky Point just after 8.30 a.m. I went outside to greet her.

She got out, smiled across at me and then spent a moment looking around at the view. 'How wonderful!' she called, waving both arms expansively.

'Good morning!' I told her happily, always pleased to see someone glad to be here. 'No navigation problems?'

She shook her head. 'Not one. You're good at instructions.'

I hoped that wasn't a barbed comment and invited her in for coffee.

'Do we have time?'

'Plenty. Come on in.'

She seemed as interested in the interior of my cottage as she had been in the exterior. 'Have you lived here long?' she asked.

'A few years. I inherited the cottage and since then I've spent a large part of my life and fortune fixing it up. Sometimes I've wondered if the sea would claim it before the work was finished.'

'You are a bit close to the edge, aren't you.'

'And the edge creeps closer every year.'

'I hope it stops soon. You've done such a good job,' she said admiringly. 'And it's such a wonderful location.'

'You're my kind of visitor,' I told her.

I made the coffee. We sat round the kitchen table with it and discussed tactics.

'If the objective is to find out what they do at this place,' Jac said, 'it might be best if I just go along as your companion.'

'And not declare your special knowledge, you mean?'

She nodded. 'It might make them overly defensive.'

'I'm glad you've suggested that. I was thinking along the same lines.'

What I didn't tell her was that I had a slightly different agenda. I wanted to see if that damned blue car was there, as well as see what Meridion House was about.

Plus, of course, I wanted to know more about the links between the art centre, the boat and the tunnel, as well as about this man Borovsky.

There was also Bill Peart's warning to fit into the mix. National security? Something was going on, and I wanted to know what it was. For the moment, the girl who had come out of the night to my door could wait; she had enough of my food to keep her going for a while.

Jac was right, though. This Borovsky guy

would likely be on the defensive if he thought he was being looked over by an art gallery owner. In fact, he might not even be prepared to let us in if he knew who Jac was.

'Is this an old fisherman's cottage?' Jac asked as we went out to my Land Rover.

'No. The other one is, but this was an ironstone miner's cottage. There were a few of them here until the cliff receded, and they went with it.'

I waved at Jimmy, who had come out of his front door to see what all the fuss was about.

'The old guy over there, is a fisherman. Or he was. Doesn't do much these days, but he's the end of a long family line of fishermen. Mostly,' I added, 'he watches out for me these days.'

Jac laughed and gave him a wave. Jimmy raised a hand in acknowledgement.

'What's his name?'

'Mack, Jimmy Mack. He's just come out of hospital,' I added. 'So now we look after each other.'

'You can't have much to do,' Jac said, 'in a tranquil place like this.'

I just grinned and ushered her into the Land Rover.

'How exciting!' she exclaimed. 'I've never been in one of these before.'

I winced and hoped I could get it started.

Meridion House appeared in my sights once again. So did the same gatekeeper. This time, though, he raised the barrier and nodded me through.

Jac looked thoughtful. 'A barrier?' she said with surprise. 'We don't have anything like that outside my gallery.'

'You don't want it either,' I told her. 'Nor any barbed wire or landmines.'

'You're the expert,' she said with a grin.

I parked on the gravelled forecourt alongside a couple of very big BMWs that looked as if they had been valeted recently. By the time we had climbed out, a smartly suited young man had appeared to guide us into the house.

From a spacious hallway, we walked down a long corridor lined with large oil paintings of what looked to me like biblical scenes. Old Masters, I supposed. I was impressed. On the thick carpet our feet didn't make a sound. All I could hear, in fact, was the gentle hum of the air conditioning — climate control system, I should say.

Borovsky was waiting for us in a large modern office full of light, and with an expansive view over fields populated by sheep and a few cattle. Meridion House, I realized

126

belatedly, must be the heart of a large farm estate, as well as being some sort of art centre.

Our host, a middle-aged, heavy-set man, stood up and came round to meet us with a big smile illuminating his features. 'Mr Doy!' he exclaimed. 'And your delightful companion. Welcome to Meridion House.'

I shook hands with him. 'My friend, Miss Turnbull,' I told him, as he turned back to Jac with a look of inquiry.

I hoped she didn't mind the subterfuge. A search on the web might have brought our welcome to an end very quickly if I had given Jac's real name.

'Enchanted,' Borovsky assured her.

She simpered back at him, to my disgust. Already I didn't like the man.

He sat us down and asked our guide to arrange coffee. 'Now,' he said, 'I understand you would like to know something of what we do here at Meridion House?'

'Very much. It's just natural curiosity,' I told him. 'Someone surprised me the other day, saying there was an art centre here. I live nearby, up at Risky Point, but I hadn't even heard of it.'

He shrugged apologetically. 'Security, I'm afraid. We have some very valuable artwork here. So I had a choice. I could fortify

Meridion House as if it was the Louvre or I could keep things quiet and simple. I chose the latter course, partly because that is more in my nature but also because I never intended this to be a public gallery. We don't want lots of visitors here. That is not what we are about.'

'It's a lovely old house, Mr Borovsky,' Jac said diplomatically. 'I think you made the right choice.'

He inclined his head gracefully.

I wondered about his origins. He was some sort of European, obviously, but was he really Russian? I should have asked Bill Peart if he could confirm what the dog walker on the beach had told me.

'What is it you do here?' Jac added. 'What is your purpose? Is it to hold and protect a private collection?'

'No, no. I am fortunate enough to have a wonderful collection, I admit, but my main purpose is to train a new generation of painters of excellence. Basically, Miss Turnbull, this is an art school, a private training facility.'

'Oh?' she said with apparent surprise.

I decided to intervene before she said anything to suggest prior knowledge — or she asked to see his teaching certificate.

'So, you have students here?'

'We do. We have students. Not many, perhaps. Not like the big art schools. But that is because we pursue excellence. Only the very best of the best young artists are invited here.'

He rattled on a bit about how wonderful and extraordinarily gifted his students were while we sipped our coffee.

'Where do your students come from?' I asked him.

'Far and wide,' he assured me. 'Wherever my scouts identify true talent.'

'Abroad even?'

'Most certainly. Yes, we do have foreign students.'

It was news to me. I hadn't heard of any foreign students coming to stay in the area. Mind you, that wasn't so surprising. I hadn't even heard of Meridion House being an art centre until the other day.

But the information chimed with something Jimmy Mack had said. He had muttered about foreigners in the vicinity. Perhaps they were some of Borovsky's students.

'Some from your own country, perhaps?' I heard Jac ask gently.

He chuckled. 'My own country, Miss Turnbull? What is my own country? Please tell me. I would like to know.'

Wisely, Jac just shrugged. I held my breath, wondering if hers was a question too far.

'I will tell you what I know,' Borovsky said with apparent good humour. 'I was born in what is now Moldova, one parent Romanian and the other Ukrainian. My father was Jewish. I grew up in Russia. For many years I lived in the United States. Now I live here some of the time, or aboard my yacht. If ever I had a country, it was the Soviet Union. But that no longer exists. So what is my country now?'

That sounded like a good question. I could understand his dilemma.

'How extraordinary!' Jac said, her face registering astonishment. 'You are indeed a citizen of the world.'

Borovsky laughed. I relaxed. He wasn't bothered by her question. He was secure in his status and standing, and confident about it.

'The world is more complicated now than when I was born, Miss Turnbull.'

He glanced at his watch and added, 'I wonder if you would like me to show you around Meridion House now?'

'Yes, please,' I said quickly, before he changed his mind.

He took us through a couple of studios where three or four young people were

130

working at easels. One looked Chinese. The others could have been from anywhere in Europe. They declined to be interrupted. We passed by quietly.

Then he showed us a few paintings in his collection. They were housed in a very discreet gallery in the secure heart of the house. I could tell Jac was fascinated, and perhaps envious.

That was it. He announced then that he had an appointment to keep and was sorry he couldn't spare us more time, but he hoped we had found our visit interesting.

'Oh, yes!' Jac said with enthusiasm. 'It's wonderful what you are doing here. I never dreamt there was such a place.'

I added my own thanks, careful not to overdo it. I knew nothing about art, I told him sincerely, but I, too, admired what he was doing here.

Once again, he inclined his head gracefully and smiled at our appreciation. Then he personally led us outside to the Land Rover, which he looked at with interest.

'I restored it myself,' I told him. 'This is my 'Old Master'.'

He laughed and congratulated me. 'Such a good job you have done, Mr Doy. It reminds me of my army days!'

We shook hands.

Just before I climbed into the vehicle, my pulse began to race. A blue Passat was now parked on the other side of the BMWs. I took a step back and looked at the rear wheel. A mudflap was missing.

'It looks like you have more visitors,' I said as easily as I could manage.

Borovsky turned, looked at the car and said, 'No, not visitors. They are men who are doing some maintenance work here.' He shrugged and added, 'I must remind them to park at the back of the house. Only visitors are supposed to park here.'

He waved us away as I set off towards the exit.

'In a word?' I said, after we had safely passed the barrier and the man in his gatehouse.

'In a word,' Jac said decisively, 'he's a phoney.'

I nodded with satisfaction.

20

Back at Risky Point, I led the way inside and we sat down again. 'Right,' I said. 'Explain yourself. Let's hear what you learned from that visit.'

Jac shrugged. 'I don't know what he's up to, of course, but nothing he told us makes much sense. You can't just run a private art school. Not unless all your students are royalty from somewhere like Saudia Arabia, and money's not a problem for them — and you're so private you don't need licensing. As for scouting the world for extraordinary young talent, well . . . that's just nonsense.

'Also,' she added, 'at least some of his Old Masters are fakes, whether he knows it or not.'

'Really?' I was surprised by her certainty. 'What makes you say that?'

'Do you recall that Rembrandt he's so proud of? Well, the real one is in the Hermitage in St Petersburg. I saw it there last year.'

'Perhaps they've sold it?'

'The Hermitage?' She chuckled and shook her head. 'No way! Some of the others were fakes, too. I'm sure of it.'

'Not stolen?'

'Well . . . It's funny you should say that.'

'I'll make some coffee,' I said.

★ ★ ★

'So what's he doing?' I murmured reflectively.

Jac sipped her coffee and shook her head. 'No idea, but it's an interesting question.'

'Maybe he's just running art holidays for rich foreigners?' I suggested. 'You know — come and paint with us on the beautiful North Yorkshire coast! Bed and breakfast, and jacuzzis in every room.'

'It's possible, but in that case you would expect them to publicize what they're doing, wouldn't you? They would have to do some marketing.'

'Probably. Unless Meridion House is so select they don't need to. Or they don't need the money. Borovsky has a big yacht as well, moored at the jetty in Port Holland.'

'Has he now?' She fluttered her eyelids. 'My kind of guy!'

I smiled, thinking Jac would look perfectly at home on a big yacht. She was made for it.

She glanced at her watch. 'I'm sorry, Frank. I must leave you. I have an appointment I must keep. But it's been an

134

interesting morning. Thank you for inviting me.'

'Thanks for coming. You've given me a lot to think about.'

She smiled. 'You must visit me sometime.'

'I'd like that. Where do you live?'

'Redcar. Like your friend Jimmy, I'm at the end of a long line of fisher folk. He'll know my father and grandfather, as well as a lot of others in the family. The Picknetts are true Redcar people, and an old fishing family.'

'Not artists?'

'Fisher folk,' she said firmly. 'I'm the black sheep of the family.'

She brushed my cheek with her lips and left. I was sorry to see her go.

If she'd stayed longer, I reflected, I might have told her about the girl. I might even have wondered aloud if the girl was in any way connected to Meridion House and the national security issue. But that would probably have been a mistake. I had no wish to get Jac into trouble with Bill Peart, or with anyone else. Best to keep such thoughts to myself. So, on balance, it was a good thing she had left.

★   ★   ★

135

Back to business. Meridion House. Borovsky. What on earth was going on? I couldn't make it out.

The best I could come up with was still the lingering thought that the place was some sort of haven for rich, young foreigners with indulgent parents who fancied having a go at painting. Maybe even for kids from Russia, and the bits that had fallen off the old Soviet Union to become separate countries. It would make sense. From what he'd told us, Borovsky would know his way around that part of the world.

By now there must be lots of oligarchs anxious to park their offspring offshore, somewhere safe — safer than home, anyway. It can be dangerous to be the child of a suddenly rich, dubiously rich father, especially if you come from a country where lots of people have scores to settle and kidnapping for ransom is a big and dangerous business.

Then there was the way that Bill Peart had been warned off on grounds of national security. What the hell did that mean? Was Borovsky under investigation, or was he running some sort of clandestine operation approved of by the authorities in this country?

There was also the blue car, and the men that went with it. Maintenance men? I didn't think so. If they had any role at all at Meridion House, then Borovsky was either in trouble or deep into something shabby.

Instinct told me Borovsky was shabby. So far as I was concerned, all the oligarchs with big boats and untold wealth were shabby. But now it wasn't only prejudice that warned me about Borovsky. It was also Jac's certainty that he had fake paintings in his collection, and was passing them off as the real thing. Not for a moment did I doubt Jac's judgement. Maybe that was prejudice, as well.

I shrugged. Time would tell. Or not. Meanwhile, I had other things to concern and distract me. Like the girl. And, I thought with a smile, like Jac Picknett.

★　★　★

Bill Peart arrived with a smile on his face, too. I regarded him warily.

'Cracked it!' he said with satisfaction.

'The bodies?'

He gave me an enigmatic look and nodded.

'You never have? I don't believe you.'

'Where's the coffee?' he asked with evident self-satisfaction.

'Coming right up.'

He planted himself at the kitchen table and stared happily out of the window while I did my usual job. Proper coffee, this time. Not just instant. This was a celebration. Pity it was a bit early to bring out the bottle as well.

'I could live somewhere like this when I retire,' Bill said dreamily.

'You? You'd be bored to death.'

He shook his head. 'I would just fish all day long.'

'Except when it was raining?'

'Except then.' He turned and fixed me with his business stare. 'I knew there had to be something going on in Port Holland. I just knew it. You don't get three bodies on the beach for no reason.'

'And there was something going on?'

He nodded. 'Drugs. I guessed that, as well. We picked up a couple of local lads in Whitby who were flogging the stuff.'

'They told you what happened on the beach?'

'Not yet. But they will. Once they see there's no way out.'

My optimism evaporated. If I had brought the whisky bottle out, I would have put it back again now.

'Local lads didn't saw off three heads and six hands, Bill.'

'Maybe not, but they'll lead us to who did.'

I planted two mugs of coffee on the table and sat down.

'You don't think so?' Bill said, suddenly looking anxious.

I shook my head. 'I don't. Killing three people is big stuff. Lads flogging penny packets in Whitby won't know enough to help you much.'

'How come you know so much about it all of a sudden?' he asked, becoming aggressive.

I looked at him and said, 'You need a rest, Bill. This is getting to you. You should step back a bit, and take it easy.'

He began to sulk. The black mood was upon him. The gloom was palpable.

'I went to Meridion House this morning,' I told him.

'What for? I thought I instructed you to keep away.'

I shook my head. 'No, you didn't. I would have gone anyway. I had an invite from Mr Borovsky to look at his paintings.'

Bill looked at me suspiciously. 'Keep away, Frank. There's things going on there that neither you nor I understand.'

'Speak for yourself. Anyway, I understand some things well enough. Borovsky is trouble. He shouldn't be here. And you should be looking into it — never mind your bloody pension!'

'Aye, well,' he said with a sigh. 'Let's solve these murders first.'

'I thought you already had?'

'So did I, until you put me straight.' He finished his coffee quickly and got up to leave.

★ ★ ★

It was time to check on Jimmy again. Before I went across to see how he was doing, I looked through the kitchen. One or two more things I'd thought I had were missing: another tin of sardines, bread from the freezer again, a couple of apples.

It wasn't much. Just enough to keep a person in hiding alive a bit longer. I wondered where she was, but I thought I knew that already.

21

Not only was she alive, she was somewhere nearby.

It wasn't surprising that I hadn't spotted her. Not really. The truth was that I had been searching for a body, alive or not, out in the open. It hadn't occurred to me that I should be looking for a resourceful and determined fugitive intent on survival — and staying hidden.

I smiled again. Then I winced as a particularly violent squall hit the corner of the house and sleet or hail pattered against the windows. I didn't like to think of anyone out there on a night like this. It wasn't necessary either. If only I could contact her!

I wondered yet again who and what she was. I had very little to go on.

She was foreign. Probably European. No more than thirty. In good shape. Tough. Resilient. Brave. And running scared, very scared.

Good instincts, too, I reflected. She had known or sensed she couldn't stay and be sure of being safe with me. Exhausted and weak as she was that first night, she had known she had to get out before it was light. She had known they would come for her, whoever 'they' were.

She couldn't be far away, wherever she was. She might even have seen what had gone on here. My forays. The trashing of my house, and the assault on Jimmy Mack. But she had needed food. So she had stayed close and re-visited my house when I was away. I wondered why. Why hadn't she just taken off?

Whatever the reason, she hadn't. And she couldn't be far away. That first morning, in her condition, just before daylight came, she would have known she wouldn't be able to get far. And she must have been terrified of being caught out in the open. So she had had to find somewhere close by.

I looked out of the window and grimaced. Wherever she was, it wasn't going to be very warm or comfortable. It didn't bear thinking about. I would have to see what I could do.

★　★　★

The night had come early, and it had come before I had got round to preparing for it. The curtains were open still. I left them open and switched on one or two more lights. Then I went round the house, and packed a suitcase with clothes. Time for business. I put

142

on a suit, a clean shirt and a tie. Then I went round switching off all the lights. After that, I left and locked the door.

The Land Rover started easily enough, which pleased me more than I can say. It was an agreeable habit the old thing had developed. I let the engine run and warm up, while I scraped the windows free of ice and hoped some of the chill would be taken off the interior. It would never get truly warm inside my vehicle, which was a good additional reason to be wearing a heavy top coat as well as the layers underneath. Even wearing heavy walking boots made sense, although warmth wasn't the only or even the main reason for wearing them.

I bumped my way along the track until I hit the road. Then I turned north and drove away with a healthy roar and dipped headlights, with the wipers doing their best to keep up with the incoming sleet. I drove a mile down the road, slowed down and turned off onto a broad gravelled area where the highway authority kept piles of grit for winter conditions.

I got out, locked up and set off to walk back to Risky Point. I went the hard way, across fields and rough ground, trying to follow a track that wasn't up to much at the best of times, even in broad daylight.

It took me getting on for an hour, which I hoped would be time enough. To be honest, I wasn't prepared to give it more than that. Enough was enough on a night like this.

The track brought me closer to Jimmy's cottage than to mine. So I stood for a while in the lee of his shed and waited. Another half hour, I thought. No more.

I could see next to nothing. It was another of those really black nights, and it was colder and wetter than ever. The ground was starting to white over with sleet on top of frost, but all I could see of my place was a vague bulky shadow.

I checked my watch two or three times. Finally it was time. The half hour was up. Thank God for that!

I set out, not troubling to move cautiously now. I walked briskly across to my cottage and opened the front door without hesitation. I stepped inside, and knew instantly that my instincts had not let me down.

'Hello!' I called softly. 'You can come out now.'

★　★　★

She had stoked the stove. I could hear the kindling crackling, and I could smell it. She was here. I didn't have to look far. Even without switching on the lights I could see the shape in front of the stove.

I closed the curtains before I put any lights on. She was sitting on the floor, as close to the stove as she could possibly get, with a quilt wrapped round her. She had to be frozen.

I drew the curtains and went through to the kitchen to close the small window properly. No need to leave that wedged slightly open any longer.

She just stared defiantly at me when I returned. I smiled encouragingly and put the kettle on. I seemed to have been doing that more than usual lately. Time I moved somewhere with room service.

I took off my overcoat and threw it over the back of the sofa. Then I removed my suit jacket and stripped off my tie. I replaced them with a fleece I took from a peg near the front door.

'It's cold out there,' I said, rubbing my hands together and pulling a wooden chair close to the stove.

'I thought you had gone,' she said in a toneless voice. 'I believed I could spend some time here.'

'You were meant to think that.' I smiled and added, 'I'm pleased it worked! I'm glad you're here again.'

'You are?'

I nodded. 'I'm tired of searching for you. It's wearing me out. You didn't need to leave in the first place. I would have helped you — I did help you,' I pointed out.

'Yes,' she said, 'but I didn't know that. Also, I would have brought trouble to your door.'

I didn't bother saying that she had anyway. Instead I got up as the kettle whistled. 'Tea or coffee?'

'I like tea. Thank you.'

'Hungry?'

She shook her head.

'You must be!'

'I had some food. I . . . ' She shrugged, guessing that I knew what she had taken.

'It's all right,' I assured her. 'I know about the bread.'

'I am sorry. It was necessary.'

'I know it was.'

I made her some tea, and me some coffee. I decided to leave the question of food for now. We could come back to that.

I decided to leave most of my questions, too. This was a moment for building a link, not frightening her away again.

'Where is your car?' she asked. 'I didn't hear it return.'

'Don't worry about that. I will collect it later.'

Already I could imagine Jimmy's face as I explained this latest development. I just hoped he would see it as good entertainment.

'It is nice here,' she said after a few moments of silence.

'Nicer than outside, anyway.'

'It is your house?'

I nodded.

'You live here alone, I think.'

'Yes, I do.'

'You have no woman?'

'I live alone.'

'And the old man is your friend?'

'My neighbour and my friend, yes. That's Jimmy Mack. I'm Frank Doy.'

The way forward, I had decided, was probably not to ask questions. Ask a direct question, nothing happened. Better to let her make the running.

'You are a fisherman, too?'

'Like Jimmy? No.'

'What is your profession?'

I smiled. 'None. I have no profession.'

She looked puzzled. 'But you own a house?'

'I make a living. So I own a house.'

She considered this and then asked the next obvious question. 'How do you make a living?'

'I'm a private investigator, amongst other

things. Security consultant, as well.'

That shut her up. For a minute or two all I could hear was the howl of the wind, the rattle of sleet against the windows and blazing logs shifting inside the stove. I was just starting to think it was time to prepare some food when she surprised me all over again.

'A private investigator?' she said, articulating the words slowly. 'Is this true?'

I nodded.

'That is very interesting,' she said, looking at me afresh.

22

I waited.

'I am an artist,' she said eventually, full of lofty disdain. 'And my friend is an artist.'

That got us a bit further forward. Bells were jangling. Lights started flashing.

'An artist?' I nodded. 'So what are you doing here at Risky Point?'

'Here is called Risky Point?'

'It certainly is.'

'A strange name.'

Then she clammed up. It was amazing how she could do that. What could I do about it? How could I coerce more from her? I didn't even have any wild horses.

Then the bells and lights went into overdrive, and there was a crash as I hit the jackpot.

'Meridion House?' I said.

Her head spun round. Her eyes flashed. Her lips stayed sealed but I knew I had got there at last.

'Something to do with Meridion House?' I continued.

'I can tell you nothing,' she said.

'I know. You've already said that — several

times. Have you been there?'

Nothing.

'Do you know the people there, the man who owns it? Mr Borovsky?'

She got up.

'I can help you,' I said.

'You have helped me, but I can tell you nothing more.'

'Where are you going? You can stay here.'

'It is not safe here. They will find me.'

She moved towards the door.

'Take some more food,' I urged. 'Anything!'

She hesitated. Then she moved into the kitchen. She reappeared with a loaf of bread. She knew where to go for bread by now.

'Stay!' I urged again. 'You are safe with me.'

'Maybe. But you are not safe with me. I am dangerous.'

I shrugged. 'I can look after myself.'

'They wrecked your house already.'

'Only because I wasn't here when they came.'

'And they hurt the old man, your friend.'

'We are ready for them now. It won't happen again, I promise you. Besides, if anything more happens I will go to Meridion House for them. I know where they live now.'

'No!' She was suddenly very agitated. I

must have pressed a switch I didn't even know about.

She came back towards me and said, 'Don't go there. Please!'

I stared at her. She was genuinely upset.

'You're going to have to tell me what this is about,' I said gently. 'What more can they do to you?'

'It is not myself I am worried about,' she said bitterly. Then she collapsed into a chair and began to sob.

Frustrated, I went to put the kettle back on. While I was in the kitchen, waiting for it to boil, I tapped my fingers on the counter top and stared hard at the calendar on the wall, which was still turned to February. Then inspiration struck. I phoned Jac.

'Can you come over?' I asked.

'When?'

'Now.'

'Now?'

'Now. I've got a situation here.'

In as few words as possible, I told her about my night visitor, her disappearance, her reappearance and her apparent fear of Borovsky.

Jac didn't interrupt or, more important, laugh. 'I'll come as soon as I can,' she said.

The phone went dead even before I could thank her. Who could tell what that meant? I shrugged and put the phone down.

* * *

I returned to the living room. The tears had stopped. 'So you are an artist?' I probed gently. 'What are you doing here?'

'The problem is my friend,' she said, ignoring my question. 'They have my friend. They will kill him if I tell the police.'

'Surely not?'

'Oh, yes! And he will disappear, like the others. The police will find nothing. And then they will say I am just a hysterical student, and claim me back.'

'"They" being the people at Meridion House — Borovsky?'

She nodded. 'Not only the house. Also the ship.'

I was getting somewhere at last, one step at a time. Better not to rush her.

'What were you and your friend doing at Meridion House?'

'We are artists. We were painting.'

I nodded to encourage her. 'Students?'

'Not really. Those days are over for us. I trained at the Hermitage in St Petersburg, Misha in Moscow.'

'So what happened?'

'It is simple. We need money to start our life together, Misha and me.' She shrugged. 'Borovsky offered us it — much money. So we came.'

152

'To do what?'

'To paint.' She shrugged again, as if it were logical, common sense even. 'I paint Rembrandts. Misha is better at Picassos.'

I sat down heavily. I needed a rest after that disclosure.

'Forgeries?' I managed to say. 'This is what it's all about?'

'Not forgeries, no! They are not forgeries.' She glared at me with contempt. 'They are originals. We paint only originals, Misha and me. The others, well . . . She tailed off with an elegant shrug. Enough said.

'So they are all at it, all the students?'

'Of course.'

'And Borovsky pays you all money?'

'Plenty of money, yes. It is a good job, I think.'

I spread my hands. 'So?' I said, trying hard to enter into the spirit of the conversation. 'What is the problem?'

'The problem is if you want to stop. Misha and me, we want to stop and go home to Russia. We have enough money now to build our house, and to have babies. But Borovsky say no — you must work some more, much more.'

Her command of English suffered as she became more intense and excited, but I understood her well enough. Jac had evidently been right about the presence of forgeries in Meridion House, but neither of us had had any idea of the nature or scale of what was going on there. Industrial production, it sounded like.

'People can't stay with Borovsky for ever, surely? They must leave sometime?'

'It is true. Some people leave, and don't come back. New people arrive.'

'Did you know any who left?'

'A few, yes. My friend from St Petersburg, Anna. Also, Misha's friend from China. They left and went home.'

Did they really? Or did they end up on the beach at Port Holland?

'But he says we can't leave, Misha and me. We must work more, and make more paintings. But we don't want to work any more. So there is big problem.'

She paused and looked around. 'Your house is very nice, I think. It is how I would like my house to be, in the country.'

I just nodded, stunned by the enormity of her revelations.

★ ★ ★

She agreed to stay for a while. I was relieved about that. She seemed none the worse for her ordeal in the open but I didn't want her to venture out there again. Enough was enough. Besides, I wanted more information from her. I hoped Jac would be here soon to help me get it.

'What is your name?' I asked. That would do for a start.

She hesitated, mindful of the fact, I suppose, that information is power. 'Sasha,' she said in due course.

'Sasha? A nice name.'

She smiled and added, 'Yes. It means 'Defender of Mankind'.'

23

I went back to collect the Land Rover. Then we talked a little more. We ate a meal I prepared. Sasha had a shower. I piled wood into the stove. Then Sasha reappeared.

'Feel better?' I asked.

'Thank you, yes.'

'Now you should rest. You have had a difficult time.'

She shrugged. 'Not so difficult, I think.'

'Not cold, wet and hungry? The hut doesn't offer many luxuries.'

She glanced at me sharply.

'That is where you were staying, isn't it? The hut on the beach?'

Reluctantly, she nodded, confirming what I had suspected since my visit.

'It is yours?' she asked.

'My friend, Jimmy's. The old fisherman in the other cottage. It's his.'

She shrugged. 'It is not damaged.'

'No, of course it isn't. And we don't mind you being there. It would have been better for you to be here, but — '

'I have told you. It is too dangerous to be here.'

I let it go. She was on edge. That wasn't surprising if half of what she had told me was true. But I was still trying to assess the scale of the problem, and becoming desperate for Jac to get here. I needed help with my visitor.

'Your friend,' I said. 'Is he in danger? Immediate danger, I mean?'

'Who knows.' She shrugged again in her fatalistic way. 'Maybe they have not killed him yet, but they will soon if I do not return.'

'Then what?'

'Then they will leave in Borovsky's ship. They are nearly ready to go. They can't stay anywhere long in case they are discovered.'

I hadn't thought of that. But of course! A man with a big, fancy boat like Borovsky's doesn't have to stay anywhere long, and it might well be dangerous to do so. On the high seas he would be much safer.

All he really needed was to find somewhere ashore from time to time, somewhere quiet and out of the way where no one paid much attention to what he was doing. Somewhere exactly like Meridion House. I was beginning to understand how a man like Borovsky could have landed in Port Holland.

'Perhaps we can rescue Misha?' I said, privately thinking it would be a lot better to risk the wrath of Bill Peart and blow the whistle. After all, what were police forces for?

157

'Yes,' she said, as if the necessity and perhaps the outcome were already agreed. 'We must do that.'

I smiled to myself. *We!* I seemed to be part of the team now.

Even so, I knew that if I picked up the phone and made that call, Sasha would probably scoot out the door and disappear again. She didn't seem to have my confidence in the police, or in any other authorities.

Besides, I would then have Bill Peart to contend with, not only for waking him up at this hour but also for ignoring his instruction to keep away from anything involving Meridion House. On the whole, it seemed politic to wait. At least to think it through a bit more.

'Have you had enough to eat?' I asked.

'Thank you, yes.'

She had eaten sparingly, but with interest, selecting what she wanted. I was surprised she hadn't simply wolfed down everything in sight.

'Go to bed,' I suggested. 'Get some rest. We can talk more in the morning.'

She considered my suggestion carefully. 'With you?' she asked.

I smiled and shook my head. 'You can sleep in the same room I showed you last time. I have a girlfriend,' I added, just in case she

158

was still uncertain about my motives.

'You are very kind man,' she said with a smile of her own. 'First you let me eat all your bread. Then I don't have to sleep with you.'

She had a directness that sometimes surprised me, but just then I smiled at her again. 'Tell me that when you know me better,' I suggested.

★   ★   ★

She made her way upstairs, leaving me to ponder what she had told me. There was a lot to consider, but at least I had found her, and found her alive still. That was a huge relief.

Right then, nothing else seemed to matter very much. One way or another, her problems could be sorted — so I assured myself anyway. We would make some plans first thing in the morning.

Then the phone rang.

'Mr Doy?'

'It is, yes.'

'Now is a time for plain speaking, Mr Doy. You have the girl. We want her back.'

Borovsky!

'You have a lot of nerve. Who the hell do you think you are?'

'My men will be there shortly to collect her. Do not try to make it difficult for them.

And do not think of contacting the authorities. If you do, there will be consequences neither she nor you will like.'

The phone went dead.

★ ★ ★

I dropped the phone back on its anchor point and started pacing the room. Shit, shit, shit! How the hell did they know?

Surely they didn't have someone watching the cottage?

No, of course they bloody didn't! If they did, they would have been able to intercept her. At the very least, they would already have been here.

The answer soon came to me; it was obvious once I had recovered from the shock. They must have left some sort of eavesdropping device here — here in my home! Probably when they ransacked the place. A microphone and transmitter. Or just a simple bug.

'Was it them?'

I looked up. Sasha had appeared on the stairs.

I nodded.

'What did they want?'

'You,' I said. 'They are coming for you.'

No point hiding it from her.

'I will go.'

'No! Get dressed, but you're going nowhere without me.'

While I was talking I was unscrewing the base of the phone unit.

'What will we do?' she asked.

'I don't know.'

I put a finger across my lips and then pointed to the phone. She seemed to understand. At least, she nodded and shut up.

There was nothing in the phone. I put it back together and made a fast reconnaissance of the room, looking for anything out of place or out of the ordinary. Nothing that I could see. I cursed violently. Me, a security consultant!

I would be able to find it, whatever it was, but that would take time, time we didn't have. They could be here in quarter of an hour from Meridion House. Already five minutes had elapsed. But they were not taking her, not after all the trouble I'd already been to. I was more than adamant about that.

I was still wearing my boots. I put on a fleece and outdoor jacket. Then I grabbed the shotgun and stuffed my pockets with shotgun cartridges. I also collected my hidden Glock.

From what Sasha had told me, I couldn't risk bringing in the police now. Her friend's life would be over if I did. I could guess what

Borovsky had had in mind when he referred to consequences. So I had to deal with the problem myself, and protect Sasha while I was at it.

'Can you manage in those boots?' I asked her when she reappeared.

Then I mimed to her, telling her to get dressed.

She nodded. 'What are you going to do?' she asked, donning my sweater and parka again.

'Don't worry. I'm going to take care of this.'

She looked at me doubtfully.

'I'm good,' I told her. 'Believe me!'

'You know what you are doing?'

I nodded. But I couldn't afford to say more.

★ ★ ★

Once outside, and away from anyone listening in, I said, 'Go back to the hut. You'll be safe there.'

She shook her head. 'No. I will stay with you.'

I grimaced. There was no time for this.

'Just do what I tell you,' I snapped. 'No arguments! OK? Understand?'

She nodded.

'And if it goes badly, run like hell!'

'Do not worry about me,' she said, giving me a serious look. 'I am competent.'

I didn't know why, but I was inclined to believe her. I wasn't going to worry about her. I had enough to do and to think about. And time was pressing.

24

I started the Land Rover, drove along the track and stopped near the entrance from the main road. My short-term tactic was to hold them off as long as possible, and as far from home as possible, while Sasha got clear. Then we'd see. That might be when I called Bill Peart.

I parked at a point where the Land Rover filled the track. To either side were drops of a few feet into soggy ground. Not even a big 4 × 4 would be able to get past without shunting me out of the way.

I switched the lights off but kept the engine running. I checked the shotgun and laid it across my knees. Then I waited.

When I saw headlights approaching and heard the sound of a vehicle slowing down, I got out and walked a few paces up the track and off to the side.

The approaching vehicle turned onto the track, its headlights bouncing wildly until they lit up the Land Rover. Then it came to a stop a few yards away. It looked like one of the big BMWs I'd seen at Meridion House. Definitely not equipped for rough, cross-country travel over boggy ground.

I stepped up to the driver's door and rapped on the window with the shotgun barrel. It was hard to see who was inside the car but there were several people there.

A face turned towards me. I rapped again, harder. The window slid down. A man I hadn't seen before stared out at me.

'Back up,' I told him. 'Back up, and get out of here.'

'We have come for something that is ours,' he said in a heavily accented voice.

I shook my head. 'You've come to the wrong place. Get out while you can.'

I sensed movement the other side of him and in the back of the car. I jammed the barrel into his face, hard. 'Both barrels,' I said softly. 'In your face.'

'What do you want?'

He wasn't phased at all. Tough guy.

'This is private property. Back up and leave!'

'What are you going to do if I don't?'

I could hear the smile in his voice now.

The rear door swung open on my side. I saw a leg protrude beneath the bottom of the door. I slammed the door with my foot. A crack like a snapping stick, together with the resultant scream, suggested serious damage to the intruding leg.

'Back up!' I said again.

Nothing happened. I reached inside and pressed the button in the roof for the interior lights. I could see now there were four of them. They had come mob-handed. Two I recognized, one yowling in the back with what I hoped was a broken leg, and one in the passenger seat.

'That's better!' I said. 'Some of us have met before, haven't we?'

The guy in the passenger seat glowered at me. He must be the one who had phoned me.

'The answer to your question about my house,' I told him, 'is no. I didn't like what you did to it. I didn't like the work you did on my elderly neighbour either. So it's good to see you both again.'

I racked the shotgun, angled it slightly and pulled the trigger. The windscreen exploded. Glass everywhere. I held the barrel against the driver's face a moment, the heat from it scorching his face. Then I stepped back and pulled out the Glock.

Almost at the same time the Land Rover's headlights came alight on high beam. That was a shock but I recovered quickly and shouted at the man emerging from the far side of the car. He stopped in mid-stride.

'Get back in,' I told him.

He got back in.

'Now what?' the driver said.

'Like I said, back up.' I swung the barrel of the shotgun against the rear side window, smashing it. Then I pushed it into the driver's chest and prodded hard. 'Now!'

He reached for the gear lever and found reverse. The car began to scream backwards. I stepped out of the light and ran alongside in a pool of darkness. I could see them but they couldn't see me. More important, they had no idea how many of us there were.

Nor had I.

The BMW backed on to the road and sped off. It was a temporary reprieve. I knew they would be back. Probably very soon.

Sooner than I'd expected, in all probability. I heard the screech of brakes. When I turned round, the BMW was doing a three-point turn fifty yards down the road. It completed the turn and stopped, pointing this way. We weren't going to be able to get out by road. That was clear.

I trotted back towards the Land Rover, shielding my eyes until the high beams dipped. Sasha was in the driving seat. She slid across to the other side when I arrived.

'Thanks,' I said. 'But you weren't supposed to be here. What happened?'

'You needed help,' she said simply. 'I knew you did.'

I let it go. We didn't have time to debate might-have-beens and what-ifs. We had to get out, and fast.

25

They would be back. And soon. I didn't have any doubt about that. They would regroup and return, bringing with them God knew what as reinforcements. A naval barrage from *Meridion*, perhaps? Meanwhile, we couldn't escape in the Land Rover; The BMW was effectively a cork in the bottle. They might be minus a windscreen and carrying one or two injuries, but we couldn't out-run them in the Land Rover even if they didn't bring up reinforcements.

'What will we do?' Sasha asked.

'I'm working on it.' I threw her a smile and added, 'Don't worry so much!'

She didn't smile back.

I stopped the Land Rover outside the cottage and threw the door open. The sleet had started again. And the wind was shrieking.

'We have to get out on foot,' I said. 'We can't stay here. We'd just be trapped.'

'Where will we go?'

'Back to the hut. They don't know about that. But we need to collect a few things together first.'

I expected them to return in minutes, probably with more men. There was no way I could hold them off from inside the cottage. My get-out-of-jail card was to call Bill Peart, but I wasn't quite ready to use it. The police were too far away to help and these were desperate, ruthless people. They weren't going to let Sasha's friend Misha survive to tell his tale.

For the moment, though, I wasn't thinking too much about Misha. Keeping Sasha and myself alive was a big enough challenge.

★ ★ ★

Back at the cottage I pulled a couple of rucksacks out of the cupboard and threw one to Sasha.

'We've only got a couple of minutes,' I told her. 'Go upstairs and grab any clothes you think you might need. Pack this sleeping bag as well.'

She went off without question, which was a relief. We hadn't time to debate anything.

I grabbed a sleeping bag for myself and an extra fleece. Then I started jamming food into the rucksack. Some extra cartridges for the shotgun and the Glock, as well. Matches and a knife.

'I am ready,' Sasha announced.

'Good!'

I threw her a smile. I was impressed by her fortitude. Wherever did I get the idea that young art students, or art graduates, must be soft and fearful when thrown into the real world?

'Let's go,' I added.

* * *

We were only just in time. As we left the house, I saw two vehicles turning onto the track. They would be carrying six or eight men, I assumed. We needed to move fast.

I had switched off the lights and locked the door although, if they wanted to get inside, a locked door wouldn't stop them.

I ran round the back of the house and led the way into rough ground, where there was little risk of car headlights catching us. The trouble was it was also difficult to see where we were going. The driving sleet and howling wind were one thing; the low cloud, and the darkness it brought, another. I had a head torch with me but I didn't dare use it. Still, this was my home patch. So I moved fairly quickly.

Sasha kept up with me, I was relieved to see. No whinging about the dark and the cold, or anything else. She was doing well. A tough girl.

I knew that already, of course. Doing what she had been doing the past few days, she had to be tough. Not just physically. Mentally, as well. Things hadn't got to her. Despite the fear — the sheer terror! — and the hardship, she had clung to her priorities. Misha was a lucky guy to have a girl like this rooting for him.

I hit the top of the path and we began the descent, slithering fast down slimy rock coated with sleet. Caution was out of the question. I didn't look back either. Whatever Borovsky's men might be doing at my cottage, there wasn't much I could do to stop them. Priorities again. My priorities.

A few paces down from what there was of a skyline, I paused and waited for Sasha to come to me.

'This leads down to the beach,' I told her, 'but it's not a proper path.'

'I know,' she said. 'It is the way I come.'

I shook my head and gave a wry smile. Of course she knew this way down. There was no other.

We went on, with me no longer making allowances for her. There seemed to be no need for that, no need at all.

26

That was one difficult journey, that journey in the dark. I dared not use a light even for a moment in case someone happened to be looking over the cliff at the time. So we slithered and groped our way down the track. And not once did Sasha complain. I heard her following close behind, as we clambered and slid across icy rock and floundered through wet patches of rotten shale, all the time with the wind and the sleet in our faces. But not once did I hear even a word of reproach, still less a wailed protest. This is some girl, I thought with admiration. Some woman.

We got there. We hit the beach at last. Not far to go now, thank God. Thankfully, the hut hadn't moved, and we found it in the darkness. It was almost as cold inside as out, but at least we were out of the wind.

'I'm sorry,' I said, wiping my face with my sleeve, 'but it would be better not to light the stove tonight.'

'No,' Sasha agreed. 'They might smell the smoke.'

'Exactly.' I smiled in the darkness and

pulled out a small torch that I switched on and shaded with my hand. 'You must have done this before.'

'Many times.'

Well, three or four, I thought. It wasn't that long since she had first turned up at my house.

'You did well, coming down the cliff.'

'It was not so bad,' she said with a shrug.

Tough kid, I thought again. I wondered if there were many like her, where she came from.

'Get some sleep,' I told her. 'You'll soon get warm in the sleeping bag. I'll keep watch for a while.'

No argument. She sorted herself out and got her head down. I donned my extra fleece, wrapped my sleeping bag round me and started to wait. It was going to be a long night but I couldn't risk us both being asleep at the same time. Never underestimate your enemy, someone I admired had once told me. I've always believed that was good advice.

★ ★ ★

The wind began to shriek ever louder. The sleet rattled against the hut with increasing ferocity. The sea roared and did its best to compete. The hut was a noisy place that night. Just as well, really. It might have been difficult to stay awake otherwise.

So I had plenty of time to consider our situation, and to wonder about my companion. Companion, colleague, victim — what was she, really? She certainly wasn't a normal victim, and no frightened young woman either. I was beginning to think Sasha was a bit special. Russian art schools must be formidable places if they produced graduates like her.

There were other possibilities beginning to edge into my mind during that long night but I resisted them. The time might well come when I would let them into the full glare of my consciousness, but not yet. We needed each other too much.

All the same, there were still things I couldn't get my head around. One question was, why were Sasha and her friend Misha so important to Borovsky? Sasha seemed to think it was because she and Misha were great painters. They made him money, presumably. So he didn't want to let them go. Could that really be the answer, though — all of it?

But I could appreciate the nature of the equilibrium between them. Borovsky couldn't dispose of Misha because Sasha would then be free to tell everything to the authorities.

With the aid of the most expensive lawyers he could hire, Borovsky might well be able to survive police inquiries, and even a court case, but it would be the end of what he was doing.

All that would change if he could get his hands on Sasha. Then he could dispose of them both without fear of consequences, if that was what he wanted. Me, too, probably. So I had to keep her out of his hands. That had to be my priority for the moment.

★ ★ ★

I don't know if Sasha really slept, but she seemed to. Then, after exactly four hours, she stirred and spoke to me.

'Everything is well?'

'So far,' I told her, trying hard to put a smile into my voice.

'Then you must sleep, and I will watch.'

I hesitated.

'You must,' she said softly. There was a rustling sound and then suddenly she was alongside me, her fingers stroking my face. She leaned down and pressed her own face against mine. 'You need sleep, too. I will watch.'

She was very persuasive. I shrugged and trapped her hand between my cheek and shoulder for a moment. 'Are you sure?'

'Of course.' She hesitated and added, 'Trust me.'

And, strangely enough, I did.

★ ★ ★

A couple of hours' sleep worked wonders for me. I came out of it ready to go. Sasha was by the window, her back to me.

'Anything?' I asked.

'I don't know,' she said over her shoulder. 'I'm not sure. Maybe I hear something. Maybe not.'

I was up and out of my sleeping bag immediately. There was nothing out of the ordinary to be seen through the window. I turned to the door and eased it open a crack. The view was of the track. I saw movement on it. I closed the door and scrambled for my things.

'Someone's coming!' I snapped. 'Get ready.'

She was already packed and set to go. She hadn't wasted her time on watch. A minute later I was ready, too. It would have taken longer if I hadn't slept in my boots.

I took another look through the door. I could see three, possibly four, figures now. They were descending the track steadily.

Another five minutes, I estimated, and they would be on the beach. I wasn't in any doubt as to who they were, and I wasn't about to hang around to discuss the weather with them.

'We will go?' Sasha said.

'We must.'

There was no way we could hold them off for long from inside a ramshackle wooden hut. With a mobile that worked down there, I might have called Bill Peart at that point. As it was, we had to get out fast — while there was still time. I grabbed my rucksack and the shotgun, and opened the door.

We broke cover and were spotted immediately. I led the way, jogging south along the beach. The tide was well in but there was still a narrow strip of firm, wet sand.

Sasha ran beside me. She had no questions, which was just as well. I needed to think ahead rather than engage in conversation. Fortunately, she seemed to understand, and there were no signs of panic for me to worry about.

We reached the end of the little beach. I looked back and saw there were four of them following us. Already they were on the sand, and perhaps only two hundred yards behind us. Too far for them to shoot, probably, and certainly out of range of my shotgun.

'We must go across the rocks and round the headland,' I shouted.

'There is a way?'

'Perhaps. I mean, yes!'

I was thinking aloud, and not altogether coherently. If we could get round the headland, there was a possibility of escape, but no certainty. Stay where we were and there was certainly a certainty. I didn't want to tell her that, though.

The tide was already raging across the rocks in front of the headland. Spray was sweeping overhead in vast, hissing sheets. I hesitated. It was too late, really. Far too late. But it was too late to go anywhere else either.

I plunged through the shallows, heading for the first of the rocks. I hoped Sasha would follow, and she did. Her confidence in me was astonishing, not that I was thinking that at the time. I was soon up to my knees, and then my thighs, in swirling water that sucked and pulled, trying to bring me down. Spray was arcing overhead in bigger sheets than ever. I glanced round. Sasha was still with me.

I went on. Now we were threading our way between large boulders, with fierce currents of seawater pulling at our legs, and sending us first one way and then another. A massive wave hit the rocks. I ducked and reached back to grab hold of Sasha's coat. We stood still, holding on until the water level receded from our chests. Then I forged on. There was no going back. Either we got through or we'd had it.

We got through.

I tramped through shallower water and made it to the beach, still hanging on to Sasha. On the sand, I doubled over for a moment, catching my breath, spitting out volumes of sea water. When I straightened up, Sasha was looking back anxiously.

'Come on!' I urged.

We started running again, heading for the next obstacle. That was the shallow depression that ran all the way up to the foot of the cliffs. I hoped to God the water wasn't too deep yet. We had to cross that hollow or we were done for. No way either back or forward then. We had to get through.

I didn't hesitate. I ploughed straight in, towing Sasha after me. Every second counted. Twenty yards to cross. The water was up to my waist, and even higher on Sasha. More waves were lining up to hit the beach. The next one would probably take the water over my head.

We made it. I hauled Sasha up out of the water onto sand. Before we started off running again I glanced back. Two of

Borovsky's men had followed us round the headland. From a distance one of them looked like part of the pair that had trashed my house and beaten up Jimmy Mack. His pal was lucky. I'd given him a broken leg, and he hadn't been able to come.

The two still following were racing towards us, with about fifty yards to go to the depression, entirely oblivious of the danger ahead. I thought of holding them up with a warning salvo from the shotgun, but that was when I realized the shotgun had not made it round the headland. The sea had taken it, and I hadn't even noticed it going.

It didn't matter anyway. They couldn't get across to us. Not any more. The surging water was too deep to wade through and too violent to swim.

They couldn't get back either now, of course.

I touched Sasha's arm. 'Come on!' I said.

She turned unquestioningly and we began to run again, jogging along the water's edge. I didn't bother looking back. There was no need. Borovsky was now two men down, if not four.

27

We weren't out of the woods yet ourselves. The beach we were now on had no way off that I had ever used or seen. Unless I could find the old route Jimmy had mentioned, we would face the same fate as Borovsky's men. I wished now I'd got him to write it down.

Sandstone, Jimmy had said. As we jogged along the beach, with sheets of water pushing us ever closer to the foot of the cliff, I was looking out for a sandstone bluff that came down to ground level — sea level, actually. I was also looking out for anywhere else where there was a possibility of getting off the beach before the tide took us.

Sasha was keenly aware of the danger, too. 'Frank, you know the way out of here?' she panted.

'I'm looking for it.'

She grimaced and shut up — for which I was grateful — and kept running.

We were halfway along the beach. So far I had seen nothing. I wouldn't say I was beginning to despair, but I wasn't far off. By now we were slapping along in shallow water. The incoming tide had used up most of the beach and was pressing us ever closer to the base of the cliff.

It was no good. I stopped running. I stood still and looked around desperately. We had no more than a couple of minutes left before we would be swimming, or washed away like the rest of the flotsam and jetsam.

Then I saw it. I'd been looking in the wrong place.

From what Jimmy had said, I had assumed the sandstone wall came down to the bottom of the cliff. But it didn't. It stopped about ten feet above the beach. It was right above us. I knew we were in the right place because I could see a couple of short iron bars protruding from the cliff face.

'This is it!' I said.

Sasha just looked at me.

'Our way off the beach.'

I pointed. She looked up, stared and then nodded. She had seen what I was pointing at. If she was unimpressed by it as a route, she didn't say so. She just looked at me expectantly.

There were no footholds, or handholds either, close to the ground. Somehow we had to get up to the first of the iron bars, ten feet above us. Anything lower down had been eroded away, leaving a sea-smoothed blank wall.

'You first,' I said. 'On my shoulders.' I

pulled off my leather belt and handed it to her. 'Drop this down for me to grab.'

Then I braced myself against the cliff wall. Sasha seemed to understand what I had in mind. She climbed onto my back, stood upright on my shoulders and then could easily reach the first of the bars.

'There is a place for my feet,' she called down.

'Good. Use it!'

I felt her weight leave me as she transferred to a thin foothold on the rock. Then I waited impatiently, sea water washing up to my waist, as she threaded the belt round the bar. I gritted my teeth against the cold and tried to ignore the big waves pounding in towards me. Soon. I knew I had to go soon.

Fully extended, the belt was a tantalizing few inches above my outstretched fingers. I tried to jump, but it was difficult in deep water. I couldn't reach the end of the belt. Desperately, I kept trying, but it was no good. I couldn't do it.

Suddenly, a boot appeared above my head, a few inches lower than the end of the belt. Sasha had taken hold of the stanchion with both hands and lowered herself until she was hanging full length. She had understood my predicament and was inviting me to use her as a human ladder.

I grasped her boot with my right hand, placed my right foot against the rock and heaved myself up so that I could catch hold of the belt with my left hand. Then I transferred my right hand to the belt, as well, taking my weight off Sasha. I was on my way, and I didn't pause until I was standing precariously alongside her on the same foothold.

Keeping tight hold of the iron bar with my left hand, I reached my right arm round her and gave her a hug to express my gratitude and appreciation. She grinned and pressed her forehead into my shoulder.

I glanced upwards and my eyes traced the route. The way ahead was now clear. The booming of the sea hitting the cliff and the lash of spray made it too noisy for conversation between us but I pointed to the holds leading upwards and urged her to go first. She didn't hesitate and began to move quickly and surely up the cliff, seemingly unintimidated by the exposure and growing drop below.

It wasn't too bad. Usually there were decent holds for either feet or hands, and if there were none there were more iron bars that some old-timer had spent precious hours cementing into holes drilled into the rock.

We made it, and at the top we both

collapsed on the ground not caring about wind, sleet, mud, or anything else for a couple of minutes. It was glad-to-be-alive time.

'You didn't warn me, Frank,' Sasha said eventually.

'About what?'

'That we would have to go mountaineering.'

'Would you have come, if I had?'

She grinned and shut up. We both knew we had been lucky.

★ ★ ★

We moved on down the coast. Just north of Port Holland we dropped down onto a little beach and sought refuge in another fisherman's hut. This one looked to be a class up from Jimmy's place — it had a lock on the door. By then, though, we were so cold and wet no lock in the world would have stopped me getting through the door. I stamped it open.

'Luxury!' I said with satisfaction, once we were inside.

And it was. A wooden table and two matching chairs. Bunk beds with bedding. A stack of logs and kindling by the stove. Even a gas hob attached to a propane cylinder.

Sasha made straight for the hob. I held my

breath and watched with interest, and with hope. Neither of us had dry matches. Sasha fiddled. The hob burst into flame; it was self-igniting.

She turned to me with a smile, even though she was shaking with cold.

'Well done!' I told her.

We were both absolutely sodden as well as dangerously cold. But now we had a flame we could fire up the wood-burning stove. I got to work. As soon as the kindling took, I started stripping off my outer clothes. I turned to Sasha to urge her to do the same, rather than sit in wet things, only to find her ahead of me. Already she was in next to nothing at all, and hanging her clothes up to dry.

'You have seen my body already,' she said with a smile. 'I have no surprises for you.'

'Oh, I don't know about that,' I said with feeling.

And I didn't. She was a bundle of surprises, one way or another. I could scarcely believe how capable she was, and how resilient in adversity. Neither fear nor hardship had thrown her off course. Altogether I thought her remarkable. And I hadn't even seen any of her paintings.

'We'll concentrate on getting ourselves a bit warmer, and drying our clothes,' I said, for the sake of something sensible to say, 'and then we'll talk about what comes next.'

'I agree,' Sasha said, for all the world as if we were taking joint decisions. 'And then we will talk some more about Misha.'

Maybe, I thought. Alternatively, we might just forget about bloody Misha — and concentrate on ourselves!

⋆ ⋆ ⋆

If we were to do anything about Misha, it seemed to me, we needed to move fast. What I had seen of the men loading crates, and what Sasha had told me, suggested pressure was building up in Borovsky's little empire.

'So something is going to happen soon at Meridion House?' I said. 'Borovsky is building up to something?'

'Yes.'

I waited but nothing more was forthcoming.

'What's he going to do?'

'Do you like me in this?'

I turned. She was wearing an old fisherman's smock in paint-spattered blue. It didn't look very clean.

I smiled. 'I liked you better before!'

She grinned and turned to continue rummaging through the heap of old clothes she had found. 'There is one for you,' she said, holding out a bundle of something in faded yellow.

'No thanks. I'll stick with what I have.'

'This is warmer than nothing,' she said, her hand smoothing the mucky old thing she was wearing. 'And it is dry.'

True, but I couldn't help thinking she didn't look as good in it.

'So what's going to happen at Meridion House?'

She shrugged. 'Borovsky will leave soon, I think.'

'Permanently, or for a holiday?'

'Permanently. He will soon have what he wants, what he is waiting for.'

'Which is?'

She just shrugged again. Perhaps she didn't know. I didn't press her. She had given me enough to think about.

But I was still in the dark. In a sense, what Sasha had just said made things worse, certainly so far as Misha's prospects were concerned. If Borovsky was ready to leave, and if he gave up on catching Sasha, I wouldn't give much for Misha's prospects.

★   ★   ★

Sasha took off the old fisherman's smock and stood smiling at me for a moment. I forgot all

189

about Misha then, when she moved towards
me and demanded that I let her into my
sleeping bag. In truth, I forgot all about
everything but her for a while. And, if
anything, she was even hungrier than me to
forget the world outside.

★   ★   ★

'You like me now?' she asked afterwards, as
we lay in each other's arms, listening to the
world going mad outside the hut.
    I smiled. 'I've always liked you.'
    'But now you like me more?'
    I laughed and squeezed her.
    'I think you do,' she said firmly. 'I am glad.
That makes me very happy.'
    It occurred to me that thoughts of Misha
didn't seem to have got in the way of Sasha's
happiness at all. But perhaps I was being
ungenerous.

★   ★   ★

We settled down for a while after that, with
food from our rucksacks and heat from the
stove. Our soggy clothes began to steam.
Outside, the wind continued unabated. Sleet
still rattled the hut from time to time. There
was no other human presence on that beach.

Thoughts of Misha did return, to me at least. We weren't far now from Port Holland. It was time to take stock and make plans. If Sasha's priority remained Misha, I had to work out a way of trying to reach and hopefully to rescue him.

'Where are they keeping Misha? Do you know?'

'I am not sure. But there are cellars.'

'Beneath Meridion House?'

'Yes.'

One of them, then. It seemed likely. Maybe I could find him. Then, if I couldn't get him out myself, I could blow the whistle and get Bill Peart's uniforms to do it.

It was a plan. Sort of. Lots of unknowns, though, stretching way back to the beginning.

'Sasha, you've never told me how you escaped. What happened that night when you first arrived at my house? How had you got away from them?'

I looked at her. She stared out of the window. I was becoming used to her now. I knew she was debating what and how much to tell me. That was irritating. We ought to have been past that point in our relationship.

'You're not my client,' I pointed out. 'You haven't hired me. I'm trying to help you — and Misha.'

She turned and smiled. 'I am sorry, Frank.

It is hard for me to accept that someone simply wishes to help me.'

Some life she must have led, was my thought.

'So?'

'They had decided to dispose of us both, like the others. So they took us north of here, along the coast. We did not know for sure what would happen, but we guessed. It was a difficult time for us.'

I'll bet! I thought. How about that for understatement?

'There were four men guarding us. They had guns. We drove, we stopped and then they made us go down to the beach with them. It was very cold but they made us take our clothes off. They laughed and said it would be easier for them if we did that. If we refused, they said, it would be more painful for us.'

She shrugged. This had to be incredibly difficult for her, but I needed to know.

'Then what?'

'They wanted to shoot us and put our bodies in a big pool. I knew that. There were four of them, and they were strong men with guns. But they were careless.

'Misha distracted them. He had warned me he would try to do something, and when he did I should be ready to run. So he pushed into two of the men. They were startled. I grabbed a gun and held it at the head of another guard.

'I ordered the others to release Misha, but they would not. Misha told me to go, to look after myself. So I did, with the guard. But first I told them that if anything happened to Misha I would go to the authorities and tell them everything. I told them to make sure Borovsky knew that.'

'So you left, taking one of the guards with you as hostage?'

'At first, but not far. Maybe twenty metres. Then we fought and he was too strong for me. The gun fell. I could either try to get it back or I could run. So I ran. I ran faster than him.'

So there it was. At last I knew now what had happened. There were still plenty of questions, but my respect for Sasha and her capabilities was, if anything, even greater.

28

'Tell me about Meridion House. Do you know anything about a tunnel, for example?'

'Yes, there is a tunnel. I have not been in it, but I know it exists. It is how they take things to the ship.'

Ah! So it did go all the way to the house.

'How many men does Borovsky have?'

'Normally, at the house there are perhaps six or eight.' She shrugged and added, 'Then there are the crew from the ship. I don't know how many.'

It added up to a lot of manpower.

'Art forgery must pay big money,' I said. 'Borovsky has a lot of wages to pay.'

She shrugged again. 'Big money, yes. It is true. There are many rich men now, not only in America. Russians, Chinese . . . They like such things — Rembrandts and Picassos. They are investments, and much safer than money in banks or shares in companies that go up and down.'

But were forged Rembrandts and Picassos such good investments? Sorry, I mean *new* original Old and Modern Masters!

'Borovsky also has other business interests,'

Sasha added, 'many interests.'

'Such as?'

'I don't know everything.'

Perhaps not, but I knew she was right in principle. A man like him really would have all sorts of business interests. He wouldn't allow himself to be totally dependent on the art market, in case all those new oligarchs stopped liking his pictures and the bottom dropped out of it.

'You really do believe he's about to leave?'

'Yes. He will go soon.'

I wondered why she thought that, and if there was a reason. No point asking her again, though. I would just get another of those shrugs.

She might have been guessing, but I felt she probably knew more than she was telling me. That was how she was. Information was leaked slowly, and grudgingly. It was hers, and she did her best to keep control of it.

★　★　★

I stepped outside for a few moments. The light was fading fast now it was mid-afternoon. Conditions had improved, though. It was still cold, but the sleet had stopped and the wind had died down.

The hut was warm when I went back

195

inside, deliciously warm. My coat hanging up above the stove felt quite dry. So did my trousers. My boots weren't bad either. I began to dress.

'What are you doing?' Sasha asked.

'I'm going to scout around a bit. See if anything's happening. I'll not be long.'

'Shall I come?'

'I'd rather you didn't. Concentrate on keeping warm and getting your clothes dry — you're going to need them eventually!'

She laughed, and I left her.

*　*　*

It wasn't much more than a mile to Port Holland. I wanted to take a look down there, to see if anything was happening. For that, I was better on my own. Besides, I needed space in my head to sort out some of what Sasha had told me. I needed to join the pieces of information together a bit better in order to make a clearer picture. Sasha might know exactly what was going on, but I certainly didn't.

And if she was right about something being about to happen, we needed to rescue Misha very quickly. If Borovsky really was planning on leaving soon, it was a safe bet that Misha wouldn't be going with him.

I started off along the beach. When I could go no further, I found a way up the crumbling cliff. I took to a footpath along the top. The old harbour came into view and I found a place where I could just sit and watch what was going on for a while. I settled in the lee of a stunted hawthorn bush. From there, I could see the jetty and *Meridion*. I could also see the entrance to the tunnel, which was closed.

Nothing much was happening. Occasionally a figure appeared on the deck of the boat. I saw a man walking his dog on the beach. A couple of little squalls blew in and made me duck my head and blink away the bits of sleet. The entrance to the tunnel stayed shut. The day faded.

Then the gloomy light began to play tricks on me. I saw movement when there couldn't reasonably be any. I blinked hard and stared. Again I saw it. Down below me, thirty or forty yards to my right, a small clump of reeds was shaking when the tall grass stalks all around were still. There was something there. Then the reeds moved, and transported themselves. They were not now where they had been.

I squinted and concentrated. It wasn't a trick of the light. The reeds had moved. I was certain of it. A rabbit? Possibly a rabbit, or a small bird. A stoat even. Something, anyway. It wasn't an illusion.

The clump of reeds moved again and then stopped. I held my breath and concentrated even harder. Now I could make out the shape of part of a man. A human shoulder? Two men, actually. One had moved sideways to be closer to the other, perhaps to confer.

I smiled with satisfaction; I knew what I was seeing. So I withdrew stealthily from my position, rejoined the track and walked on a little further. I saw no one else. No vehicle either. But that wasn't a surprise. There wouldn't be. Not close by.

Any vehicle they had would be parked up some distance away, and either hard to spot or out in the open, where it would attract no attention at all. That was how they worked. They were good at it, too, and they would be absolutely livid if they ever found out I'd spotted them, even if it was by accident.

* * *

There was no point going any further now. Sasha would be concerned about my long absence. So I turned round and set off back towards our base. Once I was a safe distance away from the cliff top I called Bill Peart on my mobile. I was surprised it was still working after its immersion in salt water.

'Can I interrupt you for a moment, Bill?'

'Sure you can. I'm happy to put this paperwork aside for a moment. What's happening?'

'Nothing much. Don't worry.'

'That's a relief!'

'Remember you warned me off the art centre?'

'I remember.'

There was suddenly a cautious note in his voice. I pressed on. 'National security, you said. Can you tell me anything more at all?'

'Is that why you've called me?'

'It would be helpful to know at least something of what's going on,' I countered. 'Is it terrorism, or what?'

'Not that.' He paused and then added, 'I can't tell you anything.'

I guessed he was being so circumspect to avoid saying anything, perhaps even just a stray word, that might cause ears to prick up.

'We spoke of one or two possibilities when the bodies were discovered. Did any of our speculation cover it?'

'It's in hand, Frank. Power and authority greater than we can bring to bear are at work. Leave it. Just leave it! Don't get in the way. You might get your nose put out of joint, or your head blown off if you do. We wouldn't want that, would we?'

All said in a light-hearted tone. All said for the benefit of someone who could overhear a conversation on a colleague's phone. Or someone who might, at a later stage, be examining the tapes of a recorded conversation. I understood.

'Have you been by my place lately, Bill?'

'Not lately, no.'

'You should call in. It's always worth a visit. You can tell me if it's still standing.'

'Why didn't I think of that? I'll take you up on it sometime.'

I switched off and hurried on. I wasn't in much doubt now about what I'd seen. National security, indeed. I'd just caught a glimpse of the SAS on the job. It doesn't come much more serious than that.

29

I had been longer than intended — too long. I hoped Sasha wasn't worried. She had been through so much in the space of a few days that that wasn't very fair. On the other hand, of course, it was her friend Misha that we were trying to rescue. Still, I couldn't reasonably expect that consideration to make her less worried.

My worries increased when I reached the hut: Sasha was gone. There was no note or anything else to suggest where she had gone, or why she had left. I gritted my teeth and scowled with frustration. I had left her alone too long. Now what?

If she had gone to look for me, she might be back soon. Her backpack was still here. So she hadn't necessarily gone for good.

Another possibility was that she had been abducted. But, looking round, I didn't think that likely. There were no signs of a struggle or forcible entry to the hut. Besides, how likely was it that Borovsky's men could have caught up with us here? Not very, in my estimation.

I dragged a chair up next to the stove and

let the heat revive my spirits while I worked out what to do next. Perhaps it was time to give Bill Peart another call.

Then the phone in my pocket began to vibrate. The screen told me nothing about the caller. Probably a landline call. I pressed the button.

'Mr Doy?'

Borovsky again!

'What do you want?'

'You have the girl still?'

'I have nobody.'

'That's a pity, if it's true. We have Miss Turnbull, or should I say Miss Picknett? I was about to suggest a trade.'

'You have — ?'

The phone went dead. I looked at the screen. Call ended. Shit! I punched the wall of the hut with frustration. Jac? God, no!

I hadn't exactly forgotten about her, but it hadn't occurred to me that she might be in danger. I had asked her to come over, but by the time she arrived at Risky Point the action should have moved on. Obviously it hadn't.

Stupid, stupid, stupid!

Christ, what now? This was the last thing I needed.

What now indeed?

Borovsky would call back, I reasoned, trying to regain some sanity. He was just testing me, putting me under pressure. He would call back.

I swore again, and wondered if what he'd said was actually true. Had he got Jac? Probably, I concluded. How else could he have got my mobile number?

Just in case he was bluffing, I phoned Jac's home. Got a recorded announcement. Left a message. Then I phoned the gallery. The receptionist said Jac wasn't available.

'Is she at work today?' I asked.

'She should be, but she isn't here at the moment. Would you like to leave a message, Mr Doy?'

'I need to speak to her. Can you ask her to give me a ring?'

'Certainly.'

That was that. If I was any further forward at all, it was only in the sense that I now knew Borovsky might well have been telling the truth. I hadn't been able to rule the possibility, or probability, out. It wasn't a bluff.

Now I would have to wait for him to contact me again. I couldn't call him. Somehow, he had engineered it so that his call to me had not left his number on my phone.

Something else was for certain. I knew now I couldn't contact Bill, after all. Involving the police might well rule out the possibility of getting Jac back alive, never mind the unfortunate Misha.

If Borovsky offered to trade, I would have to go along with him — for a while, at least. I cursed myself for ever letting Jac become involved in the first place. It hadn't seemed risky back then, but now I thought I should have known better.

★   ★   ★

But I didn't intend sitting and waiting here, in the hut. There was no reason for me to stay any longer. I had two missing now — Sasha and Jac. And somewhere there was still Misha. It was time to get off my backside and take the fight to Borovsky.

The watchers on the cliff complicated things and worried me a little. If I was right, and it was the SAS, then that justified what Bill Peart had said. National security must in some sense be at stake. But how?

For all I knew, the intelligence services might keep a watch on all foreigners with big, expensive boats. But would Bill have been warned off if they were just keeping a watching brief?

Perhaps they were about to spring into action? Perhaps, like Sasha, they believed Borovsky was building up to some sort of climax, and possibly a departure. That could explain why Bill had been warned to keep clear.

Imminent events and the need for speed could also explain why Sasha was no longer here. I wondered if she had tired of waiting and gone to try to rescue Misha herself. It would make sense, certainly to her.

I shook my head. If that was the case, there was no time for me to waste. I had to find her before she ran into trouble, and took Misha with her. I didn't want Bill to have two more bodies to add to the list. Three even, I thought grimly, thinking of Jac.

I gathered what I needed and prepared to launch out into the cold again. I wasn't taking much. I didn't actually have much with me that was useful and the Glock was missing. I'd left it with Sasha for self-defence and she seemed to have taken it with her. But I did have a knife, and I did have a small torch. I was as ready as I could be.

Then the phone vibrated and gurgled.

★ ★ ★

'You have had time to consider,' Borovsky said. 'And you have had time to check on Miss Picknett's whereabouts. So are you ready to deal?'

'Maybe. I need to speak to Miss Picknett first.'

'That can be arranged. I will call again in twenty minutes.'

I shrugged and switched off. Why did he need twenty minutes? Perhaps she wasn't there? She didn't have to be at Meridion House.

It didn't matter much where she was right now. Everything that was about to happen was going to take place at Port Holland and Meridion House. That was where I needed to be.

30

I had options, plenty of them, but none of them was a hundred per cent great. I could call the police. Bill Peart would no doubt have insisted that was my only option. The trouble was it would take time to explain, time to convince them, and time for them to get here in force — if they ever did. While all that was happening, Borovsky could exercise one of his options and liquidate the hostages, thereby removing the evidence that he had abducted them in the first place.

You could say I had lost the option to trade with Borovsky when Sasha disappeared. Not that I would have considered giving up one woman for the other, but I wasn't ruling out trading altogether.

Searching for, locating and freeing the hostages myself, by force if necessary, didn't seem a terribly practicable possibility. I would be up against a private army. But I wasn't ruling that one out either.

The more I thought about it, the more trading with Borovsky seemed a good idea. But for that to happen, I had to have something to trade with, something he wanted badly. I knew he wanted Sasha. But there must be something else. What?

Then it came to me. The best thing I could offer him was his own life. How could he turn down a trade like that? All I had to do was get close enough to make it happen.

My mind was made up. I was going for broke, for the jugular. Ignoring all Borovsky's advantages — his money and his private army — I was going to get up close and offer him a trade he couldn't refuse. I could think of no better option, for him or for me.

First, though, I was going to do some preliminary bargaining.

* ★ *

He called, on time. I was moving over the ground fast by then but I stopped and gave him my full consideration. I wanted to get it right.

'I need to speak to her,' I told him. 'I need to be sure.'

'A few words only,' he said.

There was a lull. Then: 'Frank?'

It was her.

'I'm very sorry about this, Jac. How are you?'

'So cold, Frank. The air conditioning . . . And I can't see because of the blindfold.'

I grimaced, feeling really bad. Then I tried to offer her some hope. 'Try not to worry. I'll get you out of there.'

'I know you will.'

Such faith! I swallowed hard and tried to concentrate.

Borovsky spoke next. 'Satisfied, Mr Doy?'

Satisfied? I kept cool and avoided telling him how I felt.

'Here's what we do,' I told him. 'Bring her to my house at Risky Point. We'll do the business there.'

'I assumed neutral ground would be your preference?'

'And how am I supposed to explain that to Sasha? You think I'm going to tell her she's the one losing out?'

There was a pause. I held my breath. I was taking a gamble I didn't like to think about in detail, but it had to be this way. I couldn't see how else it could work.

'Your house, then. In one hour.'

The phone went dead. I stared at it but the call had definitely ended. I glanced at my watch. The clock was running. One hour.

★ ★ ★

There would be no trade. I was sure of that. I had no illusions.

209

First, I didn't have Sasha, and even if I did have control over her I wouldn't give her up. Second, Borovsky had no intention of trading either. I was sure of that, as well. Why should he?

My guess — and my gamble, if you like — was that his men would arrive at Risky Point intending to remove both Sasha and myself from the board permanently. That would put an end to any lingering danger to himself and his operations.

Jac must be at Meridion House, I decided. That was the implication behind her clever reference to air conditioning. If she was blindfolded she couldn't see where they were but she had worked it out. Clever girl — and a brave one!

But I didn't believe she had much of a long-term future either, not by Borovsky's reckoning. Time for all of us was short, in fact. My decision to go for the man himself seemed more justified the more I thought about it.

To strengthen my hand a little, I left a message on Bill Peart's phone. I told him a group of armed men were to visit Risky Point within the hour, and I asked him to arrange for Jimmy Mack to be protected. My house, too, by implication.

Then I got moving again.

From the top of the cliff overlooking the harbour I could see Borovsky's men were hard at it. Floodlights had been set up and more heavy crates were being wheeled from the tunnel and along the jetty to the boat. People were doing things on the boat, too — getting ready to put to sea, it looked like. Sasha had been right. Borovsky was very close to departure time.

I stopped for a moment and studied a couple of the crates. I was too far away to read any markings but I began to wonder. Those long crates looked to be the wrong shape for housing works of art. I was uneasy. I had seen crates like those before. Usually they held things like rifles and machine guns.

I might be wrong. Borovsky might be no more than a dealer in forged art, but by now I doubted it. No wonder dealing out death to dissident painters came so easily to him.

Loading this stuff on to *Meridion* must be the climax Sasha had known he was working towards. But if she had known that, why hadn't she said so instead of leaving me guessing? There was no time to ponder that one.

31

The grounds of Meridion House were well protected against intruders arriving by vehicle. The gatekeeper and the heavy-duty surrounding fence saw to that. A lone man on foot was a different matter. Short of erecting coils of razor wire and turning the place into a secure compound, it could hardly be otherwise. I circled round to the landward side, stepped over the fence and got up close through the woodland to study the house itself.

There was no one on duty outside. Probably it was all hands on deck inside. Every light in the place seemed to be on. Figures crossed in front of windows that were not shielded by blinds or curtains. My guess was that Borovsky had done with Meridion House. He would not be returning. What didn't go with him would be abandoned.

While I watched, a car drew up outside the main entrance. Two suits got out and went inside. I wondered who they were. They were well-dressed men in their late thirties or early forties. It was strange. There was something out of place about them. Somehow they didn't seem to fit, although I couldn't quite put my finger on why. But obviously they knew their way around. I shrugged and moved on.

It was hard to believe that the main entrance to the house would be completely unlocked and unguarded, and even in my hurry the exposure involved in going in that way seemed too great a risk. I circled round to the back, looking for the so-called tradesmen's entrance. I found it. The door was open, with a van standing outside. Every couple of minutes a man came out to load stuff into the van.

Nothing ventured, nothing gained. I made straight for the open door and entered a kitchen just as the man doing the loading reappeared. He was carrying a painting wrapped in protective cloth. I wondered if it was one of the fakes or the real thing.

'How many more of them are there?' I asked as I stood aside for him.

'Enough,' he said, giving me a hard look.

'Need a hand?'

'Not now, no. The job's just about done.'

'OK. I'll see what the boss wants me to do next,' I said, continuing on my way.

I could feel his eyes burning into my back but I didn't look round. He wasn't sure of me. Best to keep him guessing.

I found the long corridor leading from the main entrance. Now the walls were bare. Every single one of the Old Masters was gone. It was quiet, too, the sibilant whistle of the air conditioning all that I could hear. That and my thudding heart.

Open doors revealed that most of the rooms I passed were also empty. Neither paintings nor furniture were left. Just the luxurious carpeting, and the air con that I was sure Jac had recognized. I was even more sure now that she was here. I had no idea where, of course.

Nor did I have any idea where Sasha was. For the moment I wasn't bothered about that. There were limits to what I could do for Sasha. She had made her choice, and run out on me again. There was nothing I could do about that. I just had to hope she had run in the direction of safety. If she had returned to the cauldron, to be with Misha, it was her decision.

For all of them, all three of them, my hopes of pinning Borovsky were their best hope.

★ ★ ★

I found him easily enough. He was in his office, the big room where Jac and I had met him what seemed like a thousand years ago.

214

He was sitting behind his desk, coolly administering the transfer of his establishment to the high seas. No doubt it wasn't the first time this had happened. He would know what he was doing.

If he was surprised by my appearance, he didn't show it.

'Mr Doy,' he said equably, giving me a cool look. 'How are you this evening?'

I moved fast across the room and pushed him and the swivel chair he was using back from the desk. 'Don't touch anything!' I snapped. 'Keep your hands where I can see them.'

'Tut, tut! We had a business arrangement, I thought?'

'Where is she?' I demanded.

'Miss Picknett?' He smiled. 'I could say where is Sasha.'

I pulled out my knife and pointed it at him. 'Where is she?'

He stayed cool. I give him that. He looked up at me and chuckled in my face.

'Laugh all you like,' I told him, waving the knife, 'but I want to see Jac Picknett here, with us — and alive! You're going nowhere until I see her.

'The longer we wait,' I added, 'the less chance you have of getting away. You've been under observation for some time and my guess is it won't be long before the authorities move.'

Borovsky smiled. He didn't look nervous at all. He should have been.

'You don't know what I do,' he said softly. 'You have no idea who I am, or how important I am — to both your government and mine.'

'Let's find out, shall we?' I suggested. 'Let's sit here and wait.'

A shadow of annoyance crossed his face at last. He was a busy man. This was an inconvenience. I was a nuisance.

One thing I was sure of: Borovsky could forget all his plans unless I got what I wanted. He was going nowhere. Come to that, perhaps he wasn't going anywhere anyway. I couldn't believe the SAS was going to let *Meridion* sail away into the sunset, not with the cargo I believed it was carrying. What he'd just said about his own importance was nothing but fluff.

The door swung open and crashed against the wall. I glanced round, ready to do battle. Then astonishment overcame me.

'Sasha!'

She came in carrying my Glock, held at the ready. She glanced my way but her eyes were only for Borovsky.

'I thought . . . ' I began.

'She was dead, perhaps?' Borovsky said with a chuckle. 'You are mistaken, Mr Doy. The last thing I want is to murder this young lady — either of the young ladies. Miss Picknett is my hostage, it is true, but with Sasha I wish to negotiate.'

'No negotiations!' Sasha snapped, levelling her gun.

'You are wrong,' Borovsky said. 'Even now — '

'Negotiations?' I said. 'Who with?'

Borovsky chuckled again. 'Moscow, of course. This young lady represents the Russian government. Didn't you know?'

32

My eyes bounced between Sasha and Borovsky. There was no time to process what Borovsky had just said. Sasha was raising the Glock to shoot him.

'No!' I yelled. 'Sasha, don't!'

I moved to stand in the way.

'Frank!'

'We need him,' I said. 'I need him.'

'What do you mean?'

Her face changed, took on a puzzled look.

'Don't shoot him!'

'What he means,' Borovsky said, 'is that he doesn't know where Miss Picknett is. He doesn't want you to shoot me until I have told him.'

Sasha looked even more puzzled. 'Who?'

'A client of mine,' I told her, 'and a friend. He's got her somewhere.'

'What does that mean?' she said with contempt. 'Your friend? He is my country's enemy!'

I was shocked by these revelations but I stood my ground. 'You owe me, Sasha!' I told her, reaching for the gun.

She stepped back and moved sideways, so

she could get a clear sight of Borovsky again. 'Get out of the way, Frank. I owe nobody — especially not your friend. My friend is dead.'

'Misha isn't dead,' I extemporized wildly. 'We need to find out where he is as well.'

Sasha's eyes swung back to Borovsky. 'Not dead?' she demanded. 'Is this true?'

'It could be,' Borovsky admitted with a smirk.

The smirk seemed to prove too much for Sasha. She pulled the trigger. Borovsky yelped and fell backwards, clutching his arm.

'Damn you!' I yelled, lunging for the gun.

'A flesh wound,' she told me contemptuously, hanging on to the Glock and fighting me with surprising strength.

I managed to force the gun out of her hand. It dropped to the floor. Before I could swoop to pick it up, the room was suddenly full of feet and fists. The gunshot had brought Borovsky's cavalry to the rescue.

The Glock was kicked away from me. Something hard crashed down on my head. I sprawled across the floor and took a bit of a kicking before things calmed down.

I spat out blood from a mouth injury and raised my battered head. I saw the new arrivals were no respecters of womanhood; Sasha had been knocked about, as well. She was struggling to get herself together. One of Borovsky's men reached down, picked her up bodily and hurled her into a corner of the room. Then he towered over her.

I didn't feel up to objecting on Sasha's behalf. I was in no condition to protect anybody. Besides, I was also pissed off with her. The stupid bitch! She had brought all this down on us. Now what? What the fuck was going to happen now?

Borovsky spent several minutes having his arm attended to. Then he turned back to me. By then, I was back in the land of the fully conscious.

'For your information, Mr Doy, Sasha and her colleague are agents of the FSB — not, perhaps, as infamous as the KGB, I think you will agree, but famous enough.'

I listened. I didn't nod or shake my head in case the thing dropped off. I just listened. And I knew he was speaking the truth. Things fell into place. My questions about Sasha were answered. No wonder she was tough as old boots. She was a woman with a mission — and one full of lies.

'Their role,' Borovsky said, 'was to infiltrate my organization and put a stop to my activities in the art world. The Kremlin was not truly concerned about art, not really. It was more concerned with stopping the erosion of the financial value of the collections of places such as the Hermitage, whence Sasha had come.'

'And destroying my country's culture,' Sasha contributed.

'Indeed,' Borovsky said, bowing his head in acknowledgement.

This was of limited interest to me. What was bothering me at this point was less the thought of the financial value of Russia's cultural collections and more how the hell was I going to get out of here. The future — my future, never mind anyone else's — didn't look promising.

Then something struck me. Negotiations? They had both spoken of them. That meant this game was still in progress. Borovsky hadn't finished with us yet. Otherwise, we would have been shot and fed to the fishes.

'So,' he concluded, confirming my thinking, 'now I must negotiate. These days Moscow likes to get its agents back. They are not thought so expendable as in former times. Cheer up, young lady! There is hope for you yet.'

I couldn't see any for Jac and myself, though. The Kremlin didn't have any interest in us.

'Negotiate?' Sasha snarled. 'You are dead! There will be no negotiations.'

'If only for your sake,' Borovsky said equably, 'I hope you are wrong. In any case, the world's oceans are vast. There are many places for me to go.'

★　★　★

After having heard that indisputable truth, Sasha and I were herded along corridors and down stairs, always going down. Our destination was in the cellars. A heavy timber door, studded with bolts, was opened and we were pushed inside. There, we joined Jac Picknett and a young man I took to be Misha. We had all of us arrived, together at last in one place, and so far in one piece.

33

Jac was sitting on a stone bench that might once have supported wine racks. Otherwise, the room was empty, painted white and empty, with a single light bulb hanging from the centre of the ceiling. I went straight to her.

'How are you?' I asked, taking both her hands in mine.

Startled by our arrival, she looked up and gave me a weary smile. 'Not good, Frank. I've felt better.'

She looked unharmed physically but shock had obviously taken its toll. I gave her a hug.

'They didn't knock you around?'

She shook her head. Then she rallied. 'And this is . . . ?'

'Sasha.'

'Of course! Your mystery girl.'

I turned to introduce them to each other. Sasha was still glowering at the door, as if sheer willpower could force it open. She gave Jac a perfunctory greeting.

'And this is Misha,' Jac said. 'He's Russian, too.'

'So I've been told.'

Jac was in better heart than I could ever have expected. In her own English-rose way, she was beginning to seem a tough guy, too.

I called to the man sitting on the floor in a corner. He nodded dolefully and struggled to his feet, to engage Sasha in a conversation in Russian. She responded without going overboard about it. It wasn't the reunion of childhood sweethearts, I belatedly realized. More fool me.

'So?' Jac said, looking at me expectantly.

'It's a long story,' I told her.

'So I gather.'

'Unfortunately, we got mixed up with Borovsky. Where did they pick you up?'

'At Risky Point.'

I nodded. She had arrived too late to come with us, and too early to be saved by Bill Peart.

'Explanations are going to have to wait,' I told her.

She nodded.

I turned to the young man across the cell. 'Misha?'

He came over to me. We shook hands. 'He paints Picassos,' I told Jac.

She looked impressed for a moment. Then she gave a wry smile.

'And Sasha,' I added, 'paints Rembrandts

— original Rembrandts.'

'Ah!' Jac said, as if now she understood everything. Perhaps she did.

★ ★ ★

They were colleagues, not the betrothed lovers Sasha had given me to understand. She had stood by Misha, and done what she could. But actually rescuing him had been a step too far for her. So she had focused on assassinating Borovsky. Completing their joint mission. Whatever. She still seemed amazing to me.

By now, Sasha had calmed down. She turned and came over to us. 'Miss Picknett?'

'Jac, please.'

Jac attempted a smile and got up from the stone bench where we were sitting.

'No, no! Save your strength.' Sasha looked at me and added, 'You stopped me, Frank. You should have let me shoot him.'

'You did,' I pointed out.

She shook her head impatiently. But she was quietly angry now, not angrily struggling to contain her emotions.

'What good would it have done us?' I said quietly. 'If you had killed Borovsky, his men would have killed all of us instantly. It would have been an automatic response.'

225

'But many lives would have been saved in my country.'

She turned away, leaving me wondering what she meant.

Misha explained. 'You know about us?' he asked, 'Why we are here, as art students?'

I nodded. Jac wandered off, seemingly unable to sit still and listen any more.

'That is not all,' Misha said. 'It is not everything.'

I felt like wandering off myself. This was no time for convoluted conversation about old paintings in pidgin English with someone I didn't know. I wanted to concentrate on how we could get out of here.

'He means we discovered something else,' Sasha said. 'It is not only art that Borovsky copies and smuggles.'

'No,' I agreed. 'It's guns, as well.'

Sasha was surprised for a moment. 'Yes,' she said. 'Guns, bombs, bullets. How do you know?'

'I've seen the crates they were loading onto the boat. Do you know where they are going?'

'The North Caucasus,' she said bitterly. 'Chechnya, Ingushetia and those other republics — to kill ethnic Russians.'

'We discovered this,' Misha added, as if it had been his life's work. Perhaps that's what it was now. It didn't look as if he was going to get the chance to discover much else.

'We were told to stay with Borovsky,' Sasha said. 'Our mission was to find out how the weapons were sent — by what route, and who was involved.'

That made sense. Discover the channels and then block them off. Sinking one cargo wouldn't stop the supply.

'But somehow Borovsky discovered our true identity,' Sasha added. 'So he knew what we were doing. And now he negotiates with Moscow, but it will do him no good. There will be no compromise, and no exchange.'

Again, that didn't seem to be a hopeful conclusion.

'How did he discover who you were?' I asked. 'Any idea?'

I was thinking betrayal. Money talks, and Borovsky was well able to come up with the money for bribery.

Sasha just shook her head.

'Maybe it was my fault,' Misha said slowly.

'No!' Sasha said sharply.

It didn't matter anyway. It had happened. Now we were where we were. I began to search the room, looking for a way out. One didn't immediately appear to me.

It hadn't appeared to Misha either. 'There is no way out,' he said, seeing what I was doing. 'I have looked.'

Sasha kicked the door. 'Be careful,' I told her. 'They are my good boots.'

She glowered at me. Then she changed her mind and grinned. That was better.

'Your boots?' Jac said, looking puzzled.

So to fill in some time I gave her a slightly expanded version of my previously expurgated account of recent history.

'I'm surprised you had time to consider my gallery's security requirements,' she said when I had finished.

'If that's a rebuke,' I said bitterly, 'forget it!'

'No, no! I'm just recalling what Lydia said about you having such an interesting life.'

I don't know why but that started me smiling, and that led to us both chuckling and then laughing without restraint. Hysteria, probably. Sasha and Misha looked on in total bewilderment.

★ ★ ★

We were in a stone box underground. It was a big cellar without windows or any opening other than the one filled by the heavy-duty timber door that looked as if it had been there since before the house was built. The floor was solid stone. So were the walls. The ceiling, too. All built with good, unweathered

sandstone blocks. The only opening anywhere, apart from the door, was where the
metal tube containing the cable for the
electric light came through the ceiling. That
was approximately half an inch in diameter.

My mind was racing, but going round in
ever-decreasing circles. And our situation was
desperate. I said nothing of this to the others
but I knew we had to get out of here soon, or
we wouldn't get out at all. Somehow we had
to do it.

Borovsky was wrapping things up. He was
almost ready to go. The last of his stuff must
be down at the quayside by now. There
couldn't be much more to be done up here at
the house.

And now he had us as hostages. Perhaps he
really was engaged in negotiations with
Moscow, despite what Sasha thought. It was
even possible that they might yield a result,
but it couldn't be one that included Jac and
me.

The two of us were very definitely surplus
baggage. I didn't believe for one moment that
when *Meridion* left harbour, Jac and I would
be on it. Sasha and Misha might be, God
willing, but Moscow would have no interest
at all in two Brits who had got themselves
entangled in an unfortunate situation. More-
over, to protect their own interests, there was

no way they were going to alert the UK authorities to our plight. To them, in that charming American phrase, Jac and I would simply be collateral damage.

* * *

Misha said, 'There is no way out. I have searched. It is impossible.'

Sasha gave him a look of contempt that surprised me. She had risked a lot to keep her colleague alive. Did she really hold him in such low esteem?

'Nothing is impossible, Misha,' I said gently. 'Did they not tell you that in agent training school?'

'I didn't spend long there,' he said, 'not like Sasha. Mostly I am an artist.'

Sasha shut him up then with a torrent of what sounded like rebukes in Russian. I smiled, winked at Jac and continued with my detailed examination of the cellar.

I studied the channel for the electric cable, and then I started wondering about the roof of the cellar. The ceiling was not arched. So it couldn't be stone, I realized. It must be concrete. How thick was it? Not that that mattered. We had nothing we could use as tools to find out. Also, I didn't want to interfere with the light in case something snapped or broke, and left us in complete darkness. That really would be the end.

'You're wondering if the ceiling is weak at that point?' Jac said, breaking into my thoughts.

I nodded. 'Wondering is all I'm doing. I'm pretty sure the ceiling is concrete. Probably quite thick concrete. Not that it matters much. We have no tools anyway.'

'Are we in danger, Frank? Serious danger?'

That put me on the spot. I didn't want to frighten her any more. And it was my fault that she was here. Not directly, perhaps, but through association. On the other hand, was there any point in lying?

'I think we are,' I said.

She nodded and looked thoughtful. 'So we really do have to find a way out.'

There was nothing worth adding to that. So I didn't even bother trying.

'I think you are right about the ceiling,' Jac said thoughtfully. 'It is concrete.'

I nodded weary agreement.

'Everywhere except here in the corner.'

I looked where she was pointing, and my heart started beating again. I wondered how I had missed what she'd seen.

34

Jac obviously had a better eye than me. A painter's eye. Now I looked where she was pointing, I could see what she had seen. There was a patch in the corner that was a different texture to the rest of the ceiling. Smoother, and with an edge to it. It was about eighteen inches square.

'I think it's just plaster,' she said.

I could see what she meant. Originally, something had been protruding through the ceiling, perhaps a big pipe. For some reason it had become redundant and had been removed, leaving some patchwork to be done in the ceiling.

On tip-toes I could just touch the patch with my finger ends. I scratched it. Paint flaked off, but nothing else.

I unfastened my belt buckle and pulled the belt loose from the waistband of my trousers. I reached up again and rammed a corner of the buckle at the ceiling patch. It made an impression. No doubt about it now! That wasn't concrete.

I scratched and dug again. A small piece of material detached itself and fell to the floor. I picked it up and crumbled it between my finger and thumb.

'You're right,' I told Jac. 'It is plaster.'

I turned to Misha, who was watching intently, as was Sasha.

'I can't reach very well, Misha. You're lighter than me. If you go up on my shoulders — '

He was on his feet before I had finished speaking. I stooped to let him on to my back. He took the belt and began clawing feverishly at the ceiling. A shower of plaster dust fell on me. I closed my eyes, ducked my head and concentrated on trying to stay steady.

After a few minutes I let him down. When I looked up, I could see he had made a big impression. He had exposed a piece of mesh of some sort that the plaster had been layered on.

'We should be able to just pull that down,' I said.

'Let me try,' Sasha said.

She climbed on to me and reached for the mesh. I felt her weight leave me as she clung on to the mesh and let herself drop full length.

But what we wanted didn't happen. Either it was more securely fixed than I had expected or she just wasn't heavy enough.

'Hang on!' I told her.

Then I caught hold of her round the waist and pulled down. That did it. In an avalanche of plaster and dust, the mesh and the entire plaster plug came out. I let go of Sasha and let her drop. Then we all stooped over, coughing our hearts out for a couple of minutes.

When I recovered I glanced up and marvelled at what we had created: a hole! We had created a hole wide enough even for someone like me to squeeze through.

Jac insisted that I lift her up first to see where the hole led. Why not? She deserved first go.

'It's a kitchen,' she called down softly. 'There's no one here.'

That was good enough for me. I hoisted Sasha next. Then Misha, who reached down to take my hand so that I could get up, too.

We were in an old-style kitchen, perhaps a scullery. I could see now exactly why the corner had been patched. There was a big waste pipe coming down the wall. Originally it had gone straight down into the cellar, and then, perhaps, through the cellar floor to join a drain. For some reason that arrangement had not been satisfactory. Perhaps the drain, deep underground, hadn't worked very well, causing flooding in the cellar. So the downpipe had been cut off and routed through the outside wall of the kitchen in which we now stood. Lucky for us.

I glanced round at the others. Apart from our covering of white dust, we all seemed to be in good shape. Time to get out. I had released the hostages — all three of them — and now we could make good our escape.

Wrong!

I hadn't reckoned with Sasha.

'No,' she said. 'We must go to the boat. Borovsky cannot be allowed to escape.'

'What can you do?' I said. 'He has an army of men. Better to escape and tell the British authorities. The Royal Navy can stop him.'

'We can stop him,' she insisted. 'Misha and me. It is why we are here. There is a way.'

I had known she was a fanatic. She could never have survived her ordeal otherwise. But this seemed a step too far.

'If we are lucky,' I said slowly, carefully, to avoid any misunderstanding, 'we can get out of here. If not, Borovsky will kill us all.'

Sasha shook her head stubbornly.

I looked at Misha. He seemed less gung-ho. He had been locked up for longer, and had had more time to consider his fate. Surely he knew that what Sasha was saying was madness? He spoke to her. She came back at him with an angry torrent. He backed down. That decided me.

'OK,' I said. 'We go our separate ways. You two can do what you like. Jac and I will make our own way out of here.'

I looked at Jac. She nodded agreement.

'Good luck,' I said, making for the door.

But it wasn't that easy. I should have known it wouldn't be. I should have known better.

35

My strategy was to make our way upstairs and walk out of the front door. It was disappointing that Sasha wanted no part of such a difficult and dangerous plan, but there were limits to my powers of persuasion and clearly I had reached them. So we split up and I headed for a flight of stone stairs without looking back. Jac followed me. I guessed the other way led to the entrance to the tunnel, but I didn't want to know any more about that. I'd had enough.

But by the time we reached the top of the stairs Sasha and Misha had already run into trouble. I heard sounds of struggle and then a torrent of what sounded like abuse from Sasha. It ended abruptly. I stopped and stood still, Jac beside me, and waited. I heard nothing more.

I looked at Jac and grimaced. 'Wait here,' I said. 'If I'm not back in a couple of minutes, make your way to the front door and get out. Just get out. OK?'

She hesitated.

'Do it, Jac!'

She sighed and nodded. I leaned forward

and kissed her on the cheek.

'Take care, Frank,' she whispered.

★ ★ ★

Lights had been switched off down below. The basement was very dimly lit now. Emergency lighting only, and not much of that. I edged down the stairs, wondering what I would find.

No sign of Sasha and Misha. They could have moved quickly along the corridor but I knew that wasn't it. Something had happened to them right here. I stood still for a moment, listening. I couldn't see much. Faint light from the kitchen we had just left, a yard or two along the corridor — that was about it. In the distance I could hear people doing things. Talking, the occasional shout. The screech of heavy items being pushed across a stone floor.

I stepped off the bottom step and peered into the gloom along the corridor. That was when I realized I was not alone.

A gloved hand and jacket cuff wrapped itself across my mouth and face, and pulled my head back. At the same time, something hard was jammed painfully into my back. I made no attempt to fight back. I stood still. Shocked as I was, I still had enough sense to know I was in no position to do anything but get myself shot or knifed by fighting back.

A hood was put over my head and drawn tight. What light there had been was totally gone now. I waited for the next thing to happen.

Pressure on my back started me walking. I counted my steps, all the way to thirty. Then I was made to stop. I heard a door creak open. I was pressed forward, still without a word being spoken. I heard the door close again and a key being turned.

I stood still for a few moments, waiting. Nothing else happened. I reached up and pulled the cloth bag from my head. I could see again. Not much. The light was too dim. But I could see two figures on the floor. They weren't moving.

'Sasha?' I whispered.

One of the bodies moved.

Thank God!

They had been dealt with proficiently and quickly, more so than me. Perhaps time was running out when my turn had come. I slackened the cords binding Sasha's legs and arms, and removed tape from her mouth. Then I turned to Misha.

'Thank you, Frank!' Sasha was breathless and enraged. 'Who . . . ?'

'I don't know,' I said.

But I did. I could make a good guess at who was lurking in the shadows so very secretly and efficiently. I was even beginning to guess why. Luckily, they hadn't been sure who we were, or we might not have been alive now.

It took a few minutes to free Sasha and Misha. Just as I was starting to say we had to try to get out and catch up with Jac, I heard the key turning in the lock. The door sprang open, a powerful light was shone in our faces and several armed men entered the room.

'You will come with us,' one of them said.

There was very little choice — again! We went with them.

★   ★   ★

We were taken outside and across a cobbled yard to an adjacent building that was some sort of workshop. I noted big timber benches and lots of packing material. Power tools and empty crates looked to have been in use recently. We were herded into a huge lift and pressed at gunpoint into a corner.

I contemplated making a fight of it, but not for long; the odds were not good. Besides, we still had time. If they had been going to eliminate us soon, they would have done it by

240

now. It looked to me as if we were going to discover everything we had always wanted to know about Borovsky's tunnel, and perhaps about *Meridion* as well. We were hostages again. The negotiations couldn't have finished yet.

Looking around as we emerged from the lift, it was clear that big money had been spent here. This was no ruined Victorian tunnel newly reopened after a century of disuse. Borovsky had upgraded it into a state-of-the-art highway between Meridion House and the harbour. Modern lighting had been installed. Rails had been laid, and a miniature electric train ran upon them at a fair speed.

Some of the wagons in the train were flat-bed for carrying bulky loads. But we were installed in seats on an open-top little charabanc of the kind used in modern mines. Our guards were alert and vigilant. Somehow I felt they were not the people who had captured Jac and me, and that was puzzling. These were Borovsky's men, not SAS. We had been handed over.

Whoever this lot were, it was obvious we were in serious trouble now. My one consoling thought was that there was a possibility that at least Jac was out of it. They hadn't found her. I wondered if anyone had even realized we were only three now, not four.

The little train carried only ourselves and our guards. The heavy stuff must all have gone by now. My guess was that Borovsky's departure arrangements were just about complete. What hadn't been loaded wasn't going. It was a pity that that didn't include us.

When the train stopped, there was a slight delay while one of the guards checked outside the tunnel entrance, presumably for dog walkers or surfers who might have witnessed our abduction. Then we were hustled across the beach and along the jetty to board the boat. The way *Meridion* was throbbing and bobbing about told me my guess had been correct. She was ready to launch out into the North Sea.

I thought of the clifftop watchers. Where were they? What the hell were they doing? This was when whistles should be blown and efforts made to keep the boat where it was. But there was no sign of anyone intending to interfere with Borovsky's activities.

The reason, I had to conclude, was that the SAS — and whatever higher authority was involved — had no intention of stopping or even staying Borovsky's departure. The national security interest Bill Peart had referred to must be in letting him continue without hindrance.

Why would that be? If it wasn't simply a cock-up, perhaps HMG supported what he was doing? That was a thought that gave me no comfort whatsoever. The little guy doesn't get much consideration when affairs of state take precedence.

I wondered which part of Borovsky's activities HMG liked — art or guns. Did they even know he traded in both?

★　★　★

Once aboard, we were installed in yet another prison cell. This one was below decks and pretty basic. We had exchanged a stone box for a steel box. Otherwise the facilities were the same: zero. Perhaps we wouldn't be staying long, not that I cared to contemplate that possibility.

Sasha and Misha were quiet, surprisingly so in her case. I just hoped that, like me, they were trying to figure a way out.

I caught Sasha's eye. She grinned.

'I'm glad you find something to smile about,' I said. 'Any idea what's going on?'

'Borovsky will try to negotiate with Moscow, like he said. And they will say no, no trade.'

Great.

'That doesn't sound good from our point of view, Sasha.'

'It could be worse.'

I wondered how.

'The guards will return soon,' Misha contributed.

'Oh?'

'They have gone to find rope, or something, to tie us. I heard them say.'

'Handcuffs, I think,' Sasha added.

'Oh, good!' I said, summoning all my enthusiasm for that prospect.

If they were right, we had minutes left to do something. Desperately, I wandered around our small cell. My conclusion was that without an oxy-acetelyne burner we would struggle to get out.

'Frank!' Sasha whispered.

I turned towards her. She leaned forward and pulled up her trouser leg slightly. To my astonishment, I saw the handle of a serious-looking knife sticking out of her boot.

36

I gaped at her.

'I took it from one of the guards,' she explained. 'So now we have a chance.'

Perhaps we did. Not much of one, but still a chance. We'd better make the most of it.

Before we could make any plans, the door clanged and swung open. A man stepped forward, carrying handcuffs. Two more followed him, carrying automatic weapons. The two gunmen separated quickly, giving themselves space while they covered their colleague.

The guy with the handcuffs walked past me and leaned down to snap one set of cuffs to a metal loop welded onto a steel girder. Then he moved on to another beam, and another loop.

I could see what the plan was, and I didn't like it. We were each going to be fastened by one hand to a girder. Then we were all going to be stuck here until Borovsky reached the end of his negotiations. Whatever the outcome, and whatever he subsequently decided, we wouldn't be able to do a damn thing about it.

To hell with that!

There wasn't much space in that cell, hold or whatever the correct nautical term for it was. With my back turned to the two gunmen, I took a pace and a half backwards to allow the guy with the cuffs more room to do his job. I hoped it was enough.

There wasn't much time. Two of the cuffs were already snapped into place, and the third set was being raised towards the intended steel loop. Next, in a couple of seconds, the guy placing them would probably reach for Misha's wrist, Misha being the nearest of us to him. No time left at all, really. Unfortunately, in the past thirty seconds I hadn't been able to catch Sasha's eye and warn her.

I launched myself backwards and spun round on my right foot, reaching for the nearest guard's weapon. Even before I touched it, I swung my left leg hard and caught the guard somewhere with my boot. It was his shin I hit, and probably broke. He buckled forward with pain and shock. My hands wrapped round his weapon and forced it up. His finger pulled the trigger briefly before my elbow smashed into his face. He fell backwards, with me desperately trying to pull the gun out of his hands.

Nice try, Frank, but all through the

microseconds in which the action took place I knew somewhere in my consciousness that it wasn't fast enough. The second gunman had plenty of time to respond.

But I couldn't stop now. The gun came free. From a crouched position, I launched myself bodily towards the second gunman.

I missed. He wasn't there. I hit the floor hard and rolled, crashing into the bulwark on the far side. Something was wrong. I knew it by then: I hadn't been hit.

I sprang upright, and my eyes and brain took in the scene. Then I slumped back against the wall and sucked breath back into my lungs.

'Bravo, Frank!' Sasha cried.

She was on her feet. Misha was bent over the guard who had been putting the handcuffs in place. The guy was struggling. Misha jerked his head up sharply. I heard his neck snap.

My eyes sought and found the second gunman. He was on the floor, and also not moving. I guessed a stray bullet had fortuitously found him.

I was wrong. I moved towards him but Sasha beat me to it. She reached down and pulled her knife out of his throat. Before I could do anything else, she stepped past me and sliced open the throat of the guard I had

247

hit. He wasn't going to get up again, even if his leg wasn't broken.

'That wasn't necessary,' I said, still panting heavily.

'Just in case,' she said briskly.

'Thank you, Frank,' Misha said warmly. 'You gave us a chance.'

Some art students. Why the hell had I ever been worried about either of them?

★　★　★

What next?

We had a mini-conference. Escape was pretty high on my list of priorities. I didn't know how to do it, but I was going to give it a go. Sasha had other priorities.

'We have our duty,' she informed me solemnly. 'Misha and me, we know what we must do. We must stop Borovsky.'

'We've been lucky,' I snapped. 'Let's just think about getting out of here.'

'Our mission comes first,' Misha confirmed.

'You'll die,' I said bleakly.

'If necessary,' Sasha agreed.

I felt the boat heel over as it left the jetty and began to build up speed. Soon we would be in deep water and whoever was driving this thing would really put his foot down. It was no time for disagreeing amongst ourselves.

'So what's the plan?' I asked.

'First, we kill Borovsky. Then we blow up the boat.'

'Good luck!' I said, as I headed for the door.

I didn't know if we would be able to get out of the hold, never mind do what they or I wanted to do. But staying where we were didn't seem a great idea.

'Frank!'

I paused and looked back. Sasha came towards me, a smile on her face and the knife in her hand.

I reached out and grabbed her knife hand but it was limp. She smiled and reached up to kiss me lightly on the lips. 'For everything,' she whispered. 'Thank you.'

'Yeah. You, too.' I gave her a hug. 'Coming with me?'

She shook her head. 'You go, Frank. Go!' she added, giving me a push.

I went.

37

I didn't look back. Not once. They had made their decision and I had made mine. There was no time left for reconsidering anything. It did strike me that they had got a bum deal, the pair of them. It was a suicide mission. They had to stop Borovsky and they knew there would be no negotiations on their behalf. Mother Russia still set her people terrible tasks, it seemed. God knew what chance they had of doing anything but sacrifice their own lives.

My own situation wasn't much better. The movement of the boat indicated that speed was building up. I had to get off it fast, one way or another. I headed towards the stern of the boat, thinking only that it was there that I had seen the platform that wasn't so far above the sea.

I went straight through a couple of doors and along a passageway. *Meridion* wasn't really all that big a boat. It only took me half a minute to get there.

Something must have been brewing onshore. They had taken off in a hurry and the rear end of the boat was still open. Crew members were working hard, hurriedly moving things around on the interior deck so they could get her closed up.

I walked quickly across the deck and only broke into a run when I heard the first shout. Then I ran fast — and jumped. I jumped way out to the side, hoping the boat was moving so fast it would be past me before I hit the water and gave the propellers a chance to chew me up.

Christ! It was cold. The shock hit me like a rocket. It took all the air out of me. I gasped and sank. But the propellers missed me. I knew that because I didn't feel them slicing into me.

My brain recovered from the shock. I knew what I had to do next. I kicked up to the surface and began stripping off as many of my clothes as I could. Jacket, shoes and trousers went easily. I gave up after that and started swimming towards the shore. I reckoned I had a couple of minutes before the cold dragged me down. I tried to make the best of them.

It was grim. Waves were washing around and over my head. The cold was like icicles driven into me. But I stayed focused and swam like a man possessed. Soon, though, I grew weak. The cold sapped my muscles and my brain alike. Somehow I kept going. I kept the shore in my sights and did my best.

Then I got lucky. The shore didn't seem so far away after all, and it was coming closer. Not much to do with me, I realized. The tide was running my way. It didn't really matter whether I swam or not. I would get there, but would I still be alive when I did?

★   ★   ★

It seemed like hours later when I finally crawled up onto the shingle beach. I lay full length, my face pressed into the gravel. I retched sea water out of my innards and I shook like a motor inside had gone berserk. There wasn't much left of me. I knew I was nearly done for. I raised my head and managed to crawl a few more inches up the beach, but that was all. The incoming sea lapped at my face, and I was powerless to stop it.

Then I got lucky again.

I felt myself being lifted out of the water and carried away, probably on a magic carpet. By then, I knew I was hallucinating, but I didn't care.

★   ★   ★

The next scene was real enough. There were two of them. Inside one of the fishermen's huts, they stripped my remaining clothes off me and rubbed me hard with some material that smelt like an oil rag. Then they wrapped a survival blanket round me, a tinfoil thing that seemed unlikely to do much good.

By then, my senses were returning. I noticed no one spoke for a while. I couldn't, and they didn't. One of the men lit a gas stove and heated some water, which they gave me in an enamel mug. I sipped it gratefully and felt my strength returning.

'Thanks,' I said, mustering all the words at my command.

'Bollocks! You're a fucking nuisance. I'd have left you for the crabs.'

That was nice. I looked up at him.

'Eight weeks' work wasted because of you!'

And fuck you, I thought but didn't say. SAS, I had realized by then.

'Jock!' said his mate, who was outside the hut now and had just opened the door and stuck his head in.

Jock joined him. They both stepped outside. Something seemed to be happening. I got up and shuffled to the doorway.

Way in the distance, the sky over the sea had come alive.

'Shit!' Jock said with disgust. 'That's all we need.'

A huge aurora of incredibly bright light

filled the eastern sky. Shooting stars and fiery rockets took the message even further afield. Seconds later we heard the explosion. It came rolling in on the tide, for a few moments drowning out the sound of sea on shingle.

Sasha and Misha. God bless them!

'See what you've done?' Jock said, turning to me. 'You stupid bastard!'

I looked at him for a moment. Then I hit him. I couldn't help myself. I hit him hard twice, once in the belly and once on the chin. He fell backwards, sprawling across the shingle. When he sprang back to his feet and I saw the glint of steel I knew I was in for it.

Then the one who was not Jock stepped between us and snapped, 'Leave it!'

Jock wasn't too keen to do that, but the tension drained out of the moment, sapped by the voice of command.

'Get him some clothes, so he can get out of here,' the guy in charge said.

Jock went.

The two of us who remained went back inside.

'What was that about?' the boss man asked, sitting himself down across from me.

'There were two young people I liked on that damned boat,' I told him bitterly. 'They'd been living dangerously for a long time, and they deserved better than what has just happened to them.'

He yawned. 'Get some sleep,' he suggested. 'Think yourself lucky you weren't with them.'

★ ★ ★

Surprisingly, I did sleep. When I awoke, there was a pile of clothing near me. The two SAS men were gone.

38

First, I went home. I walked, of course. No option. Anyway, it did me good. Stretched me out and got things into some sort of perspective.

For some reason best known to themselves, the SAS guys blamed me for ... what? *Meridion* blowing up? Borovsky disappearing? Or just for two months of undercover work leaving them without anything to show for it?

What would a result for them have been, for that matter? I had no idea how they looked at it.

What concerned me more was that they had stopped me getting out of Meridion House. Stopped us all. Or had they? Somebody had. But now I thought about it, that arm across my face hadn't been tough-guy bare skin, and it hadn't been swathed in camouflage or denim either. It had been smooth as silk, the cloth of an expensive suit. Who could that have been? I shrugged. To hell with it!

Personally, I wasn't unhappy that a boat load of munitions and art forgeries had been spread across the North Sea. A lot of lives had probably been saved somewhere as a result, somewhere in the North Caucasus, presumably. My regrets were all for a slim, tough Russian girl. And her boyfriend, too, if that was what he had been. It seemed so unnecessary, and a shitty end to a shitty day. The road home had never seemed so long. I felt like saying, Fuck it! and just sitting down.

★   ★   ★

My house looked the same, untouched by all the violence. I opened the front door with the spare key I kept hidden under an undistinguished stone round the back and tried to re-enter normality. It wasn't easy. My mind wasn't up to it yet. And my body ached like hell. If the SAS guy had punched me back, he would have met all the resistance of a wet paper bag.

I slumped in a chair, and sat and stared at the wall for a while. No energy left for anything else. My mind was full of disturbing pictures, mostly of the end of *Meridion* — and of Sasha and Misha. The pictures kept on coming. They were hard to stop.

But soon I started thinking of Jac, as well, and wondering if she had got out all right. I hoped to God she had. Time to start checking. If she had escaped, she would most likely have just gone home, like me.

All I got when I phoned her there was the message receiver. Jac Picknett was not available.

I tried her office next, and got another recorded announcement. I glanced at the clock on the wall and realized that wasn't surprising. Two in the morning, apparently. Where had the hours gone?

So it was late. But I was awake now, and as recovered as one could expect after a day like mine had been. I was growing more worried by the minute. Maybe Jac hadn't made it, I thought with a heart-sick judder.

The route out for her had seemed so straightforward at the time, compared with ours, but that seemed like wishful thinking now. She had had to get out of Meridion House, evade whatever security was left and then find a way of getting home in the middle of the night without money or anything else. Tricky, when you thought about it. Especially for someone who wasn't used to the life.

I heaved myself out of the chair. The adrenaline had returned. I knew what I had to do. But I wasn't walking back to Meridion House. I would kick the Land Rover until it started.

I collected a couple of things, shed the borrowed clothes and donned some of my own. I found the keys. A last glance round to check there wasn't anything else I needed.

That was when I heard a knock on the front door.

I froze. Recent events were vividly etched on my memory. In fact, they hadn't even reached my memory. They were still the present, and I was still a participant. I looked round for a weapon, and grabbed a steak knife. Then I switched off the interior lights, switched on the one over the entrance and made my way to the door.

I ought to have known better than to open the door just because someone had knocked on it. I really did. My excuse is that I was tired, exhausted even. I wasn't actually capable of thinking clearly. So I opened the door.

It flew back against me, hard. A body followed it, and fell against me, knocking me backwards. Jesus! I dropped the steak knife and clung on to the body to keep my balance.

'Frank! Thank goodness.'

Relief flooded through me. This body was fully clothed. I hung on to her. She hugged me back, even harder than I was hugging her.

'Jac!' I pulled her further inside and slammed the door shut. 'Where have you come from? I was just going to drive back to Meridion House, looking for you.'

'Jimmy's,' she said. 'I've been at Jimmy Mack's. He's lovely, isn't he?'

I might have known, I thought, shaking my head. That interfering old man!

★   ★   ★

She had got out of Meridion House without difficulty, it seemed. No one had tried to stop her. She hadn't even seen anyone.

'They were there,' I told her. 'You were lucky.'

'Who? Borovsky's people?'

'And the SAS. Maybe the SAS. A couple of them, anyway.'

She shook her head and digested that. 'Well, I never saw them.'

'Nor me,' I admitted. 'So then what?'

She had got outside and kept on walking. She had walked all the way back to Risky Point, keeping to the road. One or two vehicles had passed, but she had hidden from them. Given the time of day, or night, hitching a lift hadn't seemed a safe or sensible thing to do.

I nodded, and kept quiet.

'My feet were so sore by the time I reached Risky Point,' she said. 'I knew I had to rest. I had to find a phone. Get help, or . . . '

I steered her to the sofa. She sat down and I wrapped my arms round her. She clung to me. For a moment, I thought she was weeping. Shock had at last given way to tears. But I was wrong. She buried her face in my shoulder — and bit me!

'Hey!'

'Well,' she said, 'you deserve it. I was worried about you. And today wasn't a lot of fun.'

'I'm sorry about that.'

'Oh, it wasn't all your fault — was it?'

'Well . . . '

★   ★   ★

So she had taken refuge with Jimmy when she found she couldn't get into my house.

'You should have broken a window and climbed in.'

'Oh, I couldn't do a thing like that! What would you have said?'

I laughed. After all we'd been through, she was still capable of teasing me.

'Hot drink?' I asked. 'Or a hot bath and bed?'

She put her head on one side and looked at

me archly. 'Could we do all three — in that order?'

'Easily.'

I stood up and reached out a hand. She took it. I pulled her to her feet and kissed her. I thought she was never going to let me go.

39

In the morning, the very late morning, Jac said, 'Jimmy and I saw the explosion.'

I turned over and kissed her breast. I licked her nipple. She briefly wrapped her arm round my head and held me there, but I sensed we were in different territory now. She wanted to talk. I wasn't sure I did. I wanted the night to go on forever.

'Those young Russians,' she said. 'Was there no chance for them?'

'No. None at all.'

'The girl was so young.'

'Her choice. She knew what she was doing.'

I wasn't about to get all sentimental again about Sasha. I couldn't afford it. She shouldn't have died, but she had. Time to move on.

But it was hard to do.

★ ★ ★

We ate a long, satisfying breakfast. It wasn't necessarily what either of us would have chosen had we been in a posh hotel with a full breakfast menu, but it was fun. And it was what was available. Nutritious, too.

'Dab?' Jac said. 'For breakfast — fried dab?'

'And toast,' I pointed out. 'And as much coffee as you can drink — proper coffee.'

'I usually have fruit. Sometimes with muesli. And a glass of water.'

'Excellent!' I said with approval. 'That's what we can have every other morning — if you stay. But today we have what we can find. You've had dab before, haven't you, coming from a fishing family?'

'Yes, but not for breakfast. And not for many years. Not since I was little, and used to go out in the boat with my Uncle Edward.'

'Reacquaint yourself,' I advised.

She laughed and grabbed the handle of the skillet, just to show she could cook as well as paint.

'By the way, I will,' she said, over her shoulder.

'What?'

'Stay — for a while. Then you can come to my place.'

I smiled. Maybe I hadn't made any money out of my activities in the past week or two, but I seemed to have struck gold.

★ ★ ★

Bill Peart came to see us the next day. Well, he came to see me, actually, but Jac was there, too. He looked at her suspiciously when I made the introductions.

'Are you one of Frank's . . . clients?' he inquired gravely.

'Oh, yes,' she assured him. 'I own a gallery in Middlesbrough, and Frank has been assessing my security requirements.'

'Ah!'

He obviously recalled hearing about her, and was satisfied.

'Might we have a word in private, Frank?' he asked.

'We might. But you ought to know Jac was with me.'

He looked blank. Nothing was going to make him admit he knew what I was talking about.

'At Meridion House,' I added. 'She was with me when I spoke to Borovsky.'

Now he was really discomfited.

'She knows everything,' I assured him. 'As much as me, at least.'

His face cleared up. 'Not everything, then? Only some of it.'

'We are eager to hear anything you can add, Detective Inspector Peart,' Jac assured him, in a voice and with a smile I knew Bill would be unable to resist.

'Even I don't know everything,' he admitted, 'but . . . It's Bill, by the way.'

'Bill,' she obliged.

★ ★ ★

He knew more than me anyway. The security and intelligence agencies were furious, it seemed. Their careful surveillance over many weeks, and the intelligence gathering before that, had been kicked into touch by unanticipated events.

'Some of them no doubt involving you, Frank,' he said sternly. 'And perhaps Miss Picknett, too.'

He wasn't all that bothered himself, though, about the spy people being upset. Ordinary cops are more like normal people. They don't mind sticking a finger in the eye of higher authority from time to time. They are not terribly keen on people with guns either, whichever side they are on, and they worry a lot about The Law. That's probably a good thing — most of the time.

Borovsky, it seemed, had been spooked. Not by me, in particular. More by a chain of events of which I had only been a part.

'The bodies on the beach?' I inquired.

'Yes,' he agreed, for a moment looking pleased with himself. 'They came back to haunt him. Just when he thought he'd got rid of them.'

'The currents,' I explained for Jac's benefit. 'The bodies didn't stay in the deep pools, like they were supposed to. They fetched up on the beach at Port Holland.'

She grimaced.

'We got a result there,' Bill said, stretching it a bit. 'We discovered who was responsible for those murders.'

'Borovsky got away with it, though,' I suggested. 'You never got to charge him, did you?'

Bill shook his head. 'No, but he didn't get away with it. Nobody got off that boat. Search and Rescue didn't even find bits of bodies.'

That pretty well ruled out my last lingering hope that Sasha might somehow have escaped.

'So what else spooked him?' I asked. 'Beside the bodies, I mean.'

'Moscow, in a word. It seems they knew about some of what he was doing all along. The forgery business, I mean. They stayed their hand because they wanted to know where the forged art went when it left here.

'What seems to have led them to pull the rug out was that they found he was also shipping arms to funny places in their own country.'

'The North Caucasus?'

He nodded. 'Wherever that is.'

'The Badlands north of Georgia.'

He peered at me and said, 'You're a mine of information, Frank. You should be on Mastermind.'

I knew he didn't mean it. So I just smiled pleasantly and said, 'So what was our lot's interest?'

'Simple. They, too, wanted to know who his contacts were, but in their case it was the guns they were interested in. They didn't know about the art. They were trying to follow the guns.'

'Using the SAS?'

He hesitated and then said, 'Not only.'

Whatever the hell that meant. I raised my eyebrows.

'It's complicated.'

'Oh?'

He was enjoying this, I could tell. His inside information meant he could lord it over me.

'Go on!'

'The SAS were responsible for observation and tracking — surveillance, if you like. They were supposed to see who he passed the arms shipments to. Others — and I don't know who, exactly — had a more interventionist role.'

'Meaning they were close to Borovsky?'

He nodded.

I thought again about the mysterious figures in the shadows who had stopped our escape from Meridion House. It figured. The suits! I'd even seen them entering the building.

'So what were they after?'

'Russian spies — a spy gang. Borovsky was helping to round them up.'

I turned away for a moment, to stop myself from giggling. So there had been three groups supposedly shadowing Borovsky? Wonderful. I couldn't have made it up.

I looked at Jac. She winked — definitely a wink. Then she used a tissue to wipe her eyes.

At least Bill had given us an explanation for some funny goings on. All those people wanting to know where *Meridion* went next? No wonder they were all pissed when the damned thing blew up.

'Do your people — our people — know how Moscow dealt with it?' I asked.

He looked at me, all the usual suspicion back on his face. 'The explosion, you mean?'

I nodded.

'Not really. Or if they do, they're not telling

anyone wearing a uniform — including my chief constable.'

He paused there and studied me for a moment, head on one side, which always indicated deep-running thought processes had been activated. 'But you do?'

'I might.'

'Oh?'

'It was the Russian girl and her partner.'

'What Russian girl?'

'Sasha,' Jac said quietly.

It clicked. 'The girl we were so worried about?'

I nodded.

'She was Russian?'

Again I nodded.

After a moment a smile of pure delight lit up his face. 'Then she must have been a . . . ?'

'She was. Both of them were.'

'But . . . ?'

'They were monitoring Borovsky's activities on the art front. Moscow wanted to know who his contacts were, and where the networks ran, like you said.

'But the mission changed when guns came into it. There was no way Moscow was going to allow them to reach their destination. Sasha and her partner were ordered to stop them, any way they could — and they did.'

'So it was a suicide mission,' Bill said

slowly. He seemed lost for words for a moment. Then he said, 'Well . . . Unofficially, speaking personally, I'm sorry for the two agents — but glad they were successful.'

'My thoughts, too,' I assured him.

'And mine,' Jac added.

At times, Bill can reveal his human side.

★ ★ ★

That about wrapped it all up, at least to the satisfaction of the three of us. We were still there, having yet more coffee, when I heard heavy feet climbing the steps. The front door opened. Jimmy Mack stuck his head inside.

'Everything all right?' he asked.

'Just about,' I said.

'Come in, Jimmy,' Jac suggested. 'We have plenty of coffee left.'

'It's a little early for me,' he said wistfully.

'It's in the cupboard under the sink,' I told him. 'Help yourself.'

'Ah!' Jac said with understanding when Jimmy pulled out the Famous Grouse.

He poured himself a decent glass and accepted a small cup of coffee as a chaser. Then he looked at Bill Peart and said, 'Is this an official visit?'

Bill studied the bottle longingly and said with a sigh, 'No, but I'm still on duty.'

'That's a pity. But this might cheer you all up,' Jimmy said. He looked straight at me and added, 'Two lads from Staithes were out last night, late on, catching the tide.'

'Oh, yes?'

'They were about ten mile out,' he said complacently.

I guessed where he was going, and I held my breath.

'They were shocked by a terrible explosion. It lit up the sky and created some big waves that set their coble rocking like a wild thing. Came out of nowhere, they said.'

I stared hard, willing him to get on with it.

'Afterwards, they came across a life raft.'

'Anybody on it?' Bill asked.

'Just two people — alive. One was a girl.'

My heart was beating faster. I looked at Jac and beamed. Her hand went up to her face with surprise and delight.

'Go on, Jimmy!' I urged.

'The lads brought them ashore, a little the worse for wear but otherwise OK, they thought. Then they went for help. When they came back they were both gone, disappeared.'

I felt like clapping and hooting with joy. Jac did do some of that.

'It was her, wasn't it?' Jimmy said, looking straight at me again.

I nodded and grinned.

'We'll find them,' Bill Peart said, leaping to his feet.

'No, you won't,' Jimmy said decisively.

'No, you won't,' I agreed.

Bill paused. 'No,' he said, sitting back down. 'We probably won't.'

He looked at me and added, 'How did they do it?'

I shrugged. 'I'd only be guessing.'

'Then guess.'

'Perhaps they had explosives already planted? So all they had to do was set the timer to give them five minutes to get clear, and then abandon ship.'

'Yes,' Bill said, nodding with approval. 'That would work.'

'Brilliant!' Jac said.

'Foreigners, eh?' Jimmy Mack said, shaking his head. 'What are they like?'

'Good luck to them,' I said, reaching for the bottle to pour Jac and myself a celebratory glass apiece. I glanced at Bill. He pushed a glass forward, too.

We do hope that you have enjoyed reading this large print book.

Did you know that all of our titles are available for purchase?

We publish a wide range of high quality large print books including:
Romances, Mysteries, Classics
General Fiction
Non Fiction and Westerns

Special interest titles available in large print are:
The Little Oxford Dictionary
Music Book
Song Book
Hymn Book
Service Book

Also available from us courtesy of Oxford University Press:
Young Readers' Dictionary
(large print edition)
Young Readers' Thesaurus
(large print edition)

For further information or a free brochure, please contact us at:
Ulverscroft Large Print Books Ltd.,
The Green, Bradgate Road, Anstey,
Leicester, LE7 7FU, England.
Tel: (00 44) 0116 236 4325
Fax: (00 44) 0116 234 0205

Other titles published by
The House of Ulverscroft:

RISKY MISSION

Dan Latus

A mysterious young woman offers Frank Doy good money to drive her to a secret location in central Europe. And despite being warned off by her husband, Harry George — a dangerous Teesside gangster — Frank agrees to her request. But it's risky and the risks soon multiply. Mrs George is also taking along her two young children and a million pounds and Frank still has no idea where they are going. Meanwhile, Harry George wants — *needs* — his money back. But there's someone far more dangerous from his wife's past, who also has an interest in the money, and more . . .

NEVER LOOK BACK

Dan Latus

Living quietly in Northumberland, ex-spook Jake Ord is awakened early one morning by a sniper's bullets that only narrowly miss. It seems his old life has caught up with him. In the nearby village, MI5 agent Anna Mason catches his eye — she's on duty, but she won't reveal why . . . yet. Then as Jake thwarts an ambush, he decides he needs help and he summons Dixie, an ex-colleague and best friend of his late wife Ellie. Together, with Anna's help, they unravel an assassination plot that has political implications and confront the man they hold responsible for Ellie's untimely death.

THE CHESHIRE CAT MURDERS

Roger Silverwood

When a wild cat goes on a killing spree in the South Yorkshire town of Bromersley, Detective Inspector Michael Angel and his team's search for the animal becomes desperate. The cougar appears to be under human control and trained to kill to order. When a well-known cat enthusiast, Miss Ephemore Sharpe, becomes the prime suspect, Angel is unable to prove her guilt. However, her possession of an antique, feline pottery figure marks a decisive turn in the enquiries. But as he races to find an explanation, Angel's investigations become more mystifying and dangerous. Can he prevent more mayhem and murder?

MISCHIEF DONE

J. A. O'Brien

When nine-year-old Miranda Watts goes missing, suspicion falls on Samuel Curly, a local man responsible for the abduction of another girl some years previously. When another young girl is found dead the pressure on acting DI Andy Lukeson intensifies, but the trail goes cold when the search for Curly finds him dead. If Curly is truly innocent, as Lukeson begins to believe, then there is someone out there who knows where Miranda is, and if she's still alive . . .

THE DROITWICH DECEIVERS

Kerry Tombs

April 1890. Whilst visiting a local church-yard, the nine-year-old daughter of a prominent Droitwich businessman disappears without a trace. Detective Inspector Ravenscroft and his colleague, Constable Tom Crabb, investigate. Then, in a seemingly unconnected incident, Ravenscroft's wife, Lucy, is asked by a distraught mother to find the baby that she'd been compelled to give away. As the investigations proceed, both Ravenscroft and Lucy encounter the darkened world of Victorian child exploitation: lies, deceit and murder are commonplace — and they are stuck in a desperate race against time to save the endangered children . . .

SCENT OF MADNESS

David Wiltshire

As Lieutenant Tom O'Hara investigates several gruesome murders in a large teaching hospital, a wave of terror about the escalating severity of the situation is sweeping through the nursing staff. Despite the obscene dissection of the victims' bodies, there are forensic clues pointing to the killer. O'Hara suspects a soldier who was brought back from Afghanistan in a coma. The man is the victim of a torture he associates with the scent of roses worn by a sinister and unseen woman. The scent, unfortunately, is identical to that worn by Dr Jean Hacker, who works at the same hospital . . .